ANGEL'S FURY

GODDESSES OF VENGEANCE BOOK 1

RENEE HEWETT

MANDY ROSKO

CHAPTER

ONE

Bryony was not a villain, but she was no longer a nice girl. Not even a noble girl.

And she liked it.

Noble warriors did not break the fingers of their enemies one at a time after the white flag had been waved. They didn't revel in the screams of the pitiful creatures as they flailed and tried to escape either.

What was worse, they didn't *enjoy* it.

Yet, Bryony not only liked it, she *liked* that she liked it.

There was nothing better than serving vengeance to the scum who deserved it.

"Please, oh God, *please*," the bag of filth at her feet— who went by the name Billy online, where she'd *met* him— begged, as though invoking the name of his deity might help him in some way.

God didn't hear him. Even if the old bastard was still around, Bryony didn't think he would lend an ear to this thing at her feet.

The grub's body trembled as Bryony held on to his pinky finger—the last unbroken finger on this hand. She put just enough pressure onto it, smiling down at him with a show of pointed teeth—a little glamour to scare the fool.

He trembled, stinking of sweet and piss, his eyes dilated with animal fear, and she was happy.

He was going to do so much worse. Had already admitted to doing worse to others. He needed to pay for that. The universe wouldn't be right until he did.

"P-please..."

She added a little more pressure, his whole body tighter than a bow string.

He'd already tried fighting back. He was bigger than she was—physically. Taller, well over six feet, with more meat on his bones but with enough muscle beneath it all that any other five-foot-seven woman would likely contemplate the intelligence of confronting such a man.

He'd thought so, too.

Which was why, after she'd approached him and told him who she was and why she was there, he'd sneered at her, angry his intended victim was not there, did not exist for him to torment. He'd told her to get lost. When she didn't stop following him, he'd threatened to phone the police. Of course he wouldn't do that. When she still followed him, waiting for a private location, he attacked.

Her favorite part.

She'd led him to a remote location, away from the public space they'd met up in.

He might have thought he'd been leading her, but that was by design. He certainly wouldn't lead her back to his car. They never wanted her to get their license plates.

They never knew that wasn't what she wanted.

Bryony easily nailed him with a kick to the gut, wrenching his arm around for leverage as she flipped him over her shoulder, holding on to *just* his pinky finger to control him from going anywhere.

"Please what?"

Bryony added even more pressure on the fat little finger, testing the limits of the bone beneath the flesh, and the man's whole body trembled.

"I...I won't do it again. I swear it was the first time. I never...I never did this before."

"That's not what you said in chat."

Her lips curled even thinking of the filthy things he'd typed.

"I lied! I lied! I just wanted to make sure she was comfortable!"

They always lied. They always said it was the first time. They were never going to do it again.

They'd learned their lesson and they promised to never try this ever again.

The same story every time. She never believed them.

It was so freeing to not give a shit. To have no rules to follow but her own.

And to show these feeble humans that there were prices to pay when they crossed certain lines.

To think, all her friends said Earth was a cesspit —which, to a degree, it was—a place not worth wasting time on. How wrong they were. She really needed to get Hades and Persephone back up here. They didn't know what they were missing.

"Tell me again," she said to her captive. "What were you going to do to the girl?"

"I wasn't gonna do nothing!" Billy objected, sticking to his story. "Just talk to her."

"You drove *two hours* to *talk* to a *twelve-year-old* girl at ten at night?" She pressed a little harder, enough to make it painful, and he yowled as if she'd already broken it.

He didn't know she could do so much more with the rest of the bones in his body.

She needed him to be keep quiet, however. The public park they were in was supposed to be closed for the night, but there were rows of houses nearby, and someone might be alerted if he kept howling.

She wasn't concerned about the cameras. None

would be able to pick up on her face—a neat trick she could do as an added bonus of being a non-human on Earth. Her biggest concern was kids. Breaking curfew, sneaking out, doing things kids did. If not them, then their parents. She didn't want someone calling the police if they heard the sounds of a man in pain.

Even one as pitiful as this one.

"Th-that's all! I was just... just telling her it was wrong. That we shouldn't do this."

"Bullshit." The more he spoke, the angrier she got. "You're already vile and pathetic. The least you can do is own your dirty deeds."

"It's true! It's the truth! I'd never touch a kid!"

"Then why did you say in the chats that you wanted to *kiss* her? That you wanted to *marry* her? That she was made for you?"

There was no child in question. The person he'd been chatting with had been Bryony, setting traps for disgusting creatures like him. She set up profiles and put up the pictures using her own image, which she'd edited with different apps to make herself look younger.

Very, very young.

Then she put out the bait and waited for the predators to come and circle.

They did. Sometimes it happened fast. Sometimes it took longer.

In this case, the guy had sent her all kinds of filthy chats to read, all sorts of horrible comments and dick pics, before he was finally comfortable enough to arrange a time and place to meet the pre-teen he thought existed.

Now, Bryony was going to make sure he wished *he* didn't exist.

Billy let out a pitiful whimper.

"Answer me!" Bryony broke his finger with a satisfying crack.

He yelped so loud that time that she felt her ear drums rattle.

Bryony quickly pressed her hand to his revolting mouth, keeping the sounds muffled and stopping him before he could bring any attention to them.

She let him writhe and cry and gasp for air. When he finally calmed, she pulled her hand back.

"Now, are you going to talk, or are you ready for the next broken bone?"

"I... I didn't do nothing! It was just talk! Not... not real life, gah!"

She grabbed him by his upper and lower arm, pulling him up to standing while putting more pressure against his elbow toward the direction it definitely did not bend in.

He made a panicked noise. "P-please..."

"Isn't that what you wanted her to say?" she asked while adding a little more pressure. She shook her head. "All those disgusting messages I had to read. You're lucky. Lucky it was *me* because if I'd caught you with a *real* kid—"

"I wouldn't've *forced* her!" he shouted, as though a twelve-year-old's consent made it okay for an adult man to touch her.

In a swift move, she let go of his arms and slapped him full force across the face, sending him back down to the ground.

It was always the same with these people. Bryony didn't understand why she got angry anymore. She'd heard this at least a thousand times already.

It was never their fault. They were good people who got caught up in something they didn't mean to. It was a mistake. They wouldn't have gone through with it. They just wanted to come all this way to see if the kid was real, to tell them in person that all this was wrong.

Never mind all the nude photos, all the filthy promises for sex, pressuring the kid to make sure they didn't tell anyone about their *special relationship*.

It didn't matter how many times she met up with one of these cretins. She always got angry.

And her targets always regretted living when all was said and done.

He attempted to stand, and Bryony broke his

arm. He shrieked something nasty, a sound that reminded her of the demons of old she used to fight.

Well, Billy here was a kind of demon, she supposed. Human in form but absolutely evil in spirit, and she was going to scare the Lord right into him.

She dropped the glamor entirely, allowing him to see her horns while she unfurled her wings, which glowed gold under the park lamps, just like her hair. The light above them would cast a shadow that would make her look anything but angelic, and Billy shrieked even louder than before.

She smirked. Of course he wasn't afraid of her as long as she still had appeared mostly human. She'd beaten him up and broken his bones, but he'd still considered her a *stupid girl*. Now that he added together the pointed teeth, horns, and wings, he realized how fucked he was.

"Help! Someone help me! The devil is in the park!" Billy shouted, and Bryony didn't like that.

So, she broke his jaw.

Not that it helped. He might not have been able to enunciate words anymore, but Billy continued to wail and had already made too much noise.

She heard the siren and saw the flashing lights through the trees on the outside of the park perimeter.

Fuck. Time to hit the sky.

"I've got programs online in place, set up to track you," Bryony growled at Billy. "You even think about talking to *anyone* online—dark web included—and I'll come back for you. Don't test me. And don't forget this."

Bryony pulled out a large manilla envelope and tossed it onto the path next to Billy, who thrashed too much to notice. Then she spread her wings and jumped into the sky, heading into the trees for cover.

To her victim, she vanished into the black of night, but really, she didn't go far at all.

Bryony needed to see that the predator had been picked up. That the evidence was collected.

She watched the police arrive, watched their horror when they found her prey and was pleased to see that while one of the officers tended to Billy, calling for an ambulance, another of the men in blue —*woman* in blue, in this case—picked up the envelope and removed the stack of stapled papers Bryony had prepared for them.

Screenshots of every chat. Every photo. The cops would still need to do their research and make their own report, but this gave them a good place to start.

Billy moaned and cried through his broken jaw, practically crawling into the arms of the officer helping him. No one could understand a word he said, but she figured it was something along the lines of, *Help me, please! There's a demon woman out there!*

She'd tried in the past to correct them. Explain that she wasn't a demon or the devil, but it lessened the effect when they had to try to understand her nature.

She was, in fact, an angel. Sure, she didn't serve the heavenly father anymore—not since she walked out of heaven—and that might compel some to call her "fallen," but those in the know understood she was a fury. A vessel of vengeance and retribution who took it upon herself to ensure those who committed crimes against the natural order paid for their deeds.

Is that what had happened tonight? Had Billy really received a good amount of justice? Considering the human legal system, the creep would be out on the street soon enough. Jails were too crowded, and unless the police had a budget and authorization to do their own sting job, it was nearly impossible for them to keep people like Billy in custody for long.

Bryony could spoon-feed all the evidence in the world to them, but the system was a little too lenient on those who preyed on children, in her opinion. Which was precisely why she'd taken it upon herself in the first place.

Still, she watched. Watched the officers look over

the chats, watched them try to ask Billy about it, and then watched as an ambulance eventually came for him. The paramedics surveyed the scene before bringing a stretcher.

More flashing lights. More people. Bryony stayed in the trees.

Men like Billy were cockroaches. There were always more of them. She used to try keeping tabs on what happened to all of them after the police picked them up, but there were so damn many.

She was getting tired of it.

Normally, Bryony would have flown away by now, but for some reason, on this night, she didn't.

Bryony made herself comfortable on her branch. Maybe she was bored. Maybe she wanted to relish Billy's suffering a little longer.

The two police officers had stepped off to the side, and now two EMTs rushed from their ambulance van, all gloved and masked up, and began to assess Billy's injuries. She finally paid them more attention, looking away from Billy, one in particular catching her eye.

Wait...

All thoughts of Billy and her quest for vengeance disappeared from her mind as she zeroed in on the blond EMT. A man, and she couldn't help but feel like she'd caught sight of a ghost from the past.

Was it the shape of his jaw? The sharpness in his eyes?

Bryony squinted. She needed a better look. Right now.

She dropped from the trees, maintaining her glamor shield to keep herself invisible from the many humans now at the scene.

She crept toward the taller of the two EMTs. He wouldn't hold still. He couldn't, not with his job as he rushed back and forth from the ambulance to the stretcher, bringing any supplies he needed. Neck brace, medicine.

Bryony still watched him, taking in his features, her heart pounding in her ears.

Short-cropped, sand-colored hair, high cheekbones, and stunning blue eyes.

Eyes the color of the ocean when it was still fresh and new. Not quite immediately after creation—Bryony wasn't *that* old—but definitely before humans had come along and ruined it.

Those eyes... She'd know those eyes anywhere.

Just as she knew that brow, those cheek bones, that jawline, which even the stupid mask covering his face couldn't hide.

"Thurstan?" She didn't mean to say the name out loud, but even if she had, he *shouldn't* have been able to hear it.

Yet he paused, standing up straight, his attention

no longer focused on Billy. He looked around, as if her voice had reached him.

As though there existed a connection between them. One that transcended space and time, life and death.

She'd seen many men over the centuries with that shade of hair, with that jaw shape, with that particular brow. They were similar, but not quite the same. Always enough to catch her attention and renew an old heartbreak, but never had it been him.

This was different. He was different. Bryony couldn't breathe. She could hardly think.

It is him. It had to be. Only *Thurstan* would be able to hear her voice like this.

She raised her hand, pausing for a fraction of a moment before giving in and reaching toward his face.

After all these years, all these *centuries*, would he still feel her touch?

Before she could find out, Thurstan shook his head, breaking from the trance they'd fallen into. He stepped away from her, returning to his human duties as though anything could be more important than reconnecting with your lost love of four thousand years.

"What happened to this guy?" Thurstan asked as the cop cuffed Billy to the gurney the EMTs had placed him on.

Years of spying on the humans made this scene fairly common. EMTs, firefighters, and police usually spoke to each other if things were calm enough in the middle of...whatever they happened to be doing.

"Someone beat the shit out of him, obviously," the female officer said, pointing to Billy and swirling her finger around in the air to indicate all of Billy's wounds. Then she slapped the envelope in her hand. "The assailant left this behind."

"What is it?"

The female officer made a face. "Some real gross shit. Looks like the guy was trying to lure a kid for sex."

Thurstan hissed, making a face.

"Right?" asked the officer, in agreement. "Had to be some sort of vigilante, given the stack of evidence they'd gathered. Our victim—Billy—thought he was meeting up with a young girl and, instead, got the shit kicked out of him by some dude jacked like a UFC or MMA fighter or something."

"Fuck," Thurstan said. "Maybe the dad or another relative came and got this guy first. What happens now?"

The officer shrugged. "Now we confirm this is the actual guy and not some other perverted dipshit in the wrong place at the wrong time. He's not doing much talking and he's got no ID on him, so if this is the same guy in these photos, we check his computer and try to find out who did this to him."

"Too bad you can't let it go," Thurstan said. "Whoever did this did a community service."

"Right?" asked the officer. "Whichever guy did this deserves a medal, far as I'm concerned. It's a waste of resources trying to find the guy responsible for fucking up a predator."

Billy moaned a garbled line of attempted words —likely objecting to their assessment and trying to tell them that it was a *demon* who attacked him. Bryony smiled at his discomfort.

She didn't mind having her work's credit given to some unidentified male any more than she cared that she was always misidentified as a *demon*.

Besides, right now, she was more focused on looking at Thurstan, moving in close enough that her face was right next to his.

She longed to remove the mask from his face so she could see his nose and lips beneath the fabric.

He looked... so much the same as she remembered him.

But also different.

Of course he'd be different. Even a reincarnated angel would look different in a human form. There were some greys in his blond hair now. A few handsome crinkles around his eyes, too.

Smile lines. She hoped he'd had lots to smile about in his human life.

Thousands of years. It was a long time to miss someone, yet she never forgot him. And she never loved again.

But as she saw him now, she realized the memory of his face had faded from her mind a little. Become a bit blurry.

She could really see him now, though, and all of her memories were refreshed with his image, clear as the last day she'd seen him—the day he'd died.

Is this really possible?

Bryony glanced at the EMT's chest, at his name tag.

Tristan.

Bryony barely heard the rest of the conversation between him and the officers, but he'd clearly heard enough. Bryony could see the anger and disgust on his face when he looked at Billy.

Now, *that* was pleasing.

Time seemed to skip. Bryony was lost. Lost in time, back in the moment when she'd lost absolutely *everything*.

She didn't register the police had taped off the scene and the ambulance had driven off until she shook herself out of that horrible memory.

Did I really just see...?

Yes. She did. Hope swelled in her chest,

drowning her in its sweetness but also terrifying her in ways she hadn't known since *that* day so long ago.

It was him. She knew it was Thurstan. The sound of his voice, the look of his face. It was him.

Follow them.

Don't lose him again.

She had to see him again. The lights of the ambulance and the cruiser were still in the distance, and she needed to catch up to them before anything else happened.

Before she lost them. Before she realized that perhaps it really wasn't Thurstan.

No. It was him. It *had* to be.

Because if it wasn't, it would crush her heart in a way that would take her another ten thousand years to recover from.

Tristan and his partner, Miller, loaded Billy into the ambulance, forgoing any effort to be gentle while they checked his vitals and splinted his bones before shoving his gurney into the back of the ambulance.

The female police officer hopped in with Billy, while Tristan and Miller jumped into the front. The other officer went back to his car alone.

They rode in silence—other than Billy's occasional moans—likely everyone fuming. No one liked *helping* people like this.

Tristan hated these types of calls. He hated being called to a scene just to realize he had to bandage up someone who probably deserved what they'd gotten.

Like the man who had been beating on his wife

and she jabbed him in the face a few times with a fork, yet Tristan had to patch up Mr. Wonderful while his partner took care of the bruised and bloody Mrs.

Or the woman who had been fleeing her home after trying to murder her family. One EMT bus rushed to the family's house so they could—success-fully—save the dad and kids, while *Tristan's* ambulance had to go save murder mom, who'd wrapped her car around a pole while trying to flee.

It was rare that he knew for sure who was guilty and who wasn't in the middle of the chaos. For the most part, people were hurt, and it was his job to take care of them until they got to the hospital where doctors and nurses could take over.

And maybe the officer in the back was right. Maybe Billy, if that was his real name, was innocent in all this. It could be a guy who just looked similar to the one in the picture.

Hard to tell with his face fucked up like that.

That was what got the other EMTs through, and it was what got the police through. Innocent until proven guilty and all that.

But for some reason, Tristan usually knew.

He had a sense about these things. Like with the mother who wrapped her car around a pole after trying to run away from attempting to kill her own family.

When he'd arrived on scene, he could almost *see* she'd done *something*, like a dark, filthy cloud around her soul.

And he could see it with Billy, too.

The guy was guilty as fuck.

He'd put money on it.

He hadn't liked the job in either case, but Tristan was nothing if not a professional. He cared for anyone in need. Even the ones he didn't like.

Even Billy.

He felt nasty having been near someone like that. He wanted to go home and take a scalding hot shower now. Too bad he had hours left on his shift.

Tristan worked on their report while Miller drove them to the nearest emergency room. He made sure all the vitals were there, as well as the inventory of injuries assessed. He also added the notation that *Billy* was being escorted by the city's finest.

He checked that every T was crossed and every I dotted because he damn well didn't want to get called back for anything missing on the report. If he had to see this prick again, he might very well end up breaking the rest of his bones.

When they pulled up to the hospital, Tristan somehow managed to keep a neutral face as they unloaded the son of a bitch and passed off the report to the ER staff. He took the signatures from the police officer and the receiving doctor, and then they got the hell out of there.

"Man, wish I'd been there to see who it was that kicked the shit out of him," Miller said the moment they were back in their vehicle without patient or officer accompaniment.

"Don't think I would've minded helping whoever it was," Tristan grumbled in agreement. "But from the look of his results, not much help was needed."

"No kidding!" Miller laughed. "That guy is probably seven feet tall and jacked to hell."

"Probably. Christ." Tristan had to shudder.

"You think he did it?" Miller asked.

Tristan didn't look at him. "We don't have all the facts. The police will double check that folder they got."

"Yeah, but come on, do you think he did it?"

Tristan and Miller had worked together long enough that Miller knew about Tristan's scoreboard.

How well he could read people.

"Yeah, I think he did it."

"Damn," Miller said then laughed darkly. "If I'd been there, I would've loved to get a bowl of popcorn and watch the show. That must've been amazing."

"I think Billy's guilty, but I'm not sure anyone wants to be near whoever did that."

"You know, you sure it wasn't you? You're getting

pretty jacked," Miller said, bringing up the fact that all of his EMT teammates had been teasing Tristan for how much he'd been working out lately. Usually, they tried to connect the workouts and his lack of dating.

Tristan rolled his eyes. "Right, because I definitely had time to sneak away from my shift, beat the piss out of him, and then get back to the bus here in time for a pickup, right?"

"I'm just joking!" Miller laughed.

"Yeah, I know," Tristan said, though part of him wished he had done it. That he had the capability to get guys like that off the streets. "Did you see that stack of screenshots this dude left behind for the cops? My man must have been on that shit for months."

"Could explain why you never have any time for dating."

Tristan sighed and groaned. Yet, this was what half the job was about. Joking around with each other to distract from the heaviness of it all.

"Well, then what's your excuse?" Tristan shot back.

Miller laughed in response.

He parked the ambulance around the back of the hospital, and they both jumped out. Unlike usual dispatch stations where they waited around for calls all night, working at the hospital meant pitching in, lending a hand to doctors, nurses, and orderlies who might need it. Sometimes it was as easy as helping move someone from a gurney to a bed. Sometimes it was more adrenaline-producing, like providing CPR to a coding patient.

Miller went one way and Tristan the other while they checked their areas to see if anyone needed them, waiting for their pagers to go off.

Ex firefighters were brought in to assist with the heavier patients who needed help standing up and sitting down, moving to their wheelchairs and showers. If there weren't enough of them on hand, or if someone was sick, Tristan was called in to help in those areas. Especially now that he'd been working out.

He waited for anyone to need him so he could forget about Billy and what he was accused of.

And how he *knew* the guy was guilty before the police could even work through and double check the evidence.

Thurstan.

His entire body froze as though hearing the voice from a missing part of his soul call out to him.

He exhaled a trembling breath, something inside him warm and flaring to life.

It wasn't the first time that had happened. It happened earlier that night in the park.

His reaction to it was stronger this time.

He spun around, but no one was there in the hall. Not even a nurse. He jogged down the hallway, looking in the rooms and down the crossing halls, seeing if anyone nearby could have said it.

He saw sleeping patients through their room windows. One elderly man recovering from surgery had his TV on, but the volume was on low, and the excitement of his game show wouldn't had made Tristan's spine shiver like that.

No one looked to be talking to him.

So what had it been?

He rubbed his chest, just over his heart.

When he'd heard it in the park, there was no one around who'd seemed to have said it, either, and the others with him hadn't reacted as though they'd heard it.

But then the officer had started to tell him about the allegations against Billy, and Tristan's blood had filled with simmering rage, forgetting that cool, soothing voice, that name and all the strangeness that had come with it.

He had work to do. He couldn't be standing around in the dark halls of the hospital doing nothing.

But he couldn't move. He *listened*.

The halls were quiet, the darkness deep.

Tristan flexed his fingers. "Where are you?"

Now, as he focused, he could hear her loud and

clear. How strange. It wasn't even fully his name—it had sounded like *Thurstan* and not *Tristan*—and it wasn't the voice of anyone he knew. Yet, he could pull it up from his memory, clear as a bell, as though he'd heard it many, *many* times before.

A memory he'd almost forgotten but couldn't quite remember.

He ran his fingers through his hair, trying to get the strange idea out of his head that—even though she hadn't said *Tristan*—someone had been calling to him. Someone *important*.

Not possible. If someone had really been speaking, the others would have heard it, too. Yet no one acknowledged it.

So clearly, it had just been a strange sound that had jumped into his imagination.

He chalked it up to *déjà vu*. That had to be it. Like when one thought they'd seen or heard something before, when they knew it hadn't really happened.

The alternative? He really hoped he wasn't going to start hearing voices. Thank God he was about to have four nights off—after ten straight on. He clearly needed the break.

"Food," he muttered to himself. It was past time for him to take a break and eat something from the hospital cafeteria. Maybe that would help him hold things together until he clocked out for the day.

He was hungry, and hearing things wasn't a great explanation, but he was taking it.

Even the stale turkey sandwich and bag of chips couldn't stop him from thinking about it.

It was better than focusing on Billy, though.

Thurstan.

He closed his eyes. Where was that voice coming from?

Had he watched a TV show with a character named Thurstan? Maybe... Gilligan's Island? He couldn't quite be sure. In any case, why the phantom word in his brain now?

He wasn't the kind of guy to believe in ghosts, but right now, the way his mind was obsessing with the tone of the woman's voice, he wondered if such a thing might be true.

No, you're just overworked and overtired, he told himself as he tossed his trash and started circling the hospital again.

Why were there no pages? It wasn't usual for them to be *this* slow. Maybe Miller had bribed dispatch with some candy bars so he'd get called first to any of the menial tasks that only required one of them around the hospital.

Tristan sighed, deciding he better go show his pretty face and dole out some of his winning smiles to entertain the bored folks in dispatch if he wanted any action that night.

But as he did, a figure appeared.

Not walking down the hall toward him. Not poking out from one of the rooms on either side.

She just *materialized* right in front of him, as if she'd stepped through a thick fog but wasn't quite there.

Her lips moved, and he heard it again: *Thurstan.*

The voice and the face were both hauntingly beautiful—ethereal, more exquisite than any woman he could imagine, while also touching his soul.

As though he knew her from somewhere.

But he didn't. He couldn't recall ever seeing the golden hair, full and perfect dark lips, porcelain-perfect skin, or tortured amber eyes.

Not unless it had been in a dream he'd forgotten about a long, long time ago.

Just as she'd appeared, she was suddenly gone, leaving Tristan dazed and confused.

"Tristan, yo!"

He whirled around.

"Why are you just standing here?" Miller asked, approaching him from the opposite direction of the woman. He paused, his smile faltering. "You look like you've seen a ghost. Or a beautiful woman. Wait, was it a beautiful ghost woman?"

"Did you see her just now?" Tristan looked at

him, pointing back where she'd been. "Have you seen her before?"

Miller blinked and jerked his head back. "No, dude. I wasn't serious. You okay?"

No. He wasn't okay.

"I... Apparently, I'm just hallucinating, Miller. And, *yes,* before you say it, it's been too long, and I need to get laid if I'm imagining women."

"Was she naked?" Miller elbowed him, laughing.

"No, she wasn't naked. Fuck off!" Tristan gave him a jab and continued walking down the hallway while the two talked.

"You wanna sneak in some shut-eye in the bus? I won't say anything," Miller said. "And I'll come get you if I need anything."

"No, I'm fine. I just ate, so it should be okay." Tristan's brain scrambled to place where he'd seen her before. "It's just been a long night."

He thought of the woman's face, still absolutely clear in his mind, as though she were still there, walking next to them.

Though his eyes saw clearly that the space beside them was empty. No one walked with them. She wasn't there.

"I'm just trying to place where I saw her before," Tristan thought out loud. "A TV show or movie, I don't know."

"Probably an ad," Miller figured. "They get beautiful models, and then they photoshop them till they're more illustration than person anymore. I'm sure the woman you're fantasizing about right now is just selling toothpaste or shampoo. Come on, man. Let's get the hell out of here."

"Wait," Tristan said, finally looking at Miller and spotting the bag of candy in his hand. "Are you on your way to dispatch to charm more calls out of them?"

Miller feigned innocence, shrugging.

"Too bad they like my smile better." Tristan laughed, taking off at top walking speed to beat his co-worker to the dispatch room. "And I'm faster than you, too!"

THREE

ryony followed him around the hospital all night.

Fuck, how much of a creeper am I?

But she couldn't lose track of this man, and she also wasn't about to pop out of nowhere and say "ta-dah" or something. What if she was wrong? What if she was hallucinating? Seeing only what she wanted to see because she'd missed him so much?

Which was all kinds of wrong because she was probably making this poor bastard think the exact same thing.

Staying up late hours at a stressful job and hearing a woman calling his name would fuck with anyone's head.

But what if I'm not wrong? What if I appear, and he knows exactly who I am?

She gave it a try after he finished his lunch. She dropped her invisibility glamor and appeared to him when he turned down an empty hallway. Her heart had pounded in her chest as she waited for his eyes to round with recognition. For him to speak her name. For there to be any indication that he recognized her. *Anything.*

But he didn't. He looked shocked. He stared at her, blinking a couple of times, as though waiting for his head to clear.

He never said her name. Never looked happy to see her again.

Bryony cloaked herself again quickly when his partner appeared.

This human, Tristan, didn't know her. He looked like Thurstan, but Thurstan wasn't in there. No way, because Thurstan would have recognized her instantly.

She had to be wrong about this. *Had* to be mistaken.

She only realized how much she'd fucked it up when Tristan and his buddy started talking about ghosts.

Oh shit, I'm making him think he's being haunted, she thought. *Maybe I shouldn't make this poor guy think he's losing his mind.*

She meant to leave the hospital, to leave him

alone, but she continued to follow him without speaking or appearing to him again.

As if his very soul pulled her along by a fragile string.

She tried to spot anything in his looks or behavior that could help convince her she was wrong. Trying to snap herself out of it. Trying to figure out if she'd been a victim of tricks, some kind of mind game.

Had someone done this to her? Someone from before, her old life, who would want to play this kind of trick on her?

There wasn't a single being she could think of who would do that. She had neither friends nor enemies in the supernatural world—not anymore— though she'd made enough of them in the human world.

Any humans who hated her likely didn't know the supernatural world existed, let alone know how to contact someone who could do something like this to mess with her.

Was it some sort of toxic gas she'd flown through? No. No human-created toxin would be able to affect her. Not unless something brand spanking new came out, and she doubted there were any chemicals in the sky that could do more to her than get her a little high

Stop trying to talk yourself out of it.

Bryony gritted her teeth, her hands clenching and unclenching.

Despite everything, despite her doubts, or her wishful thinking, or her lack of any real proof, it was him.

She *knew* this was him. In her gut she knew the truth. If she shut off the stupid questioning, she *knew* it.

The second she admitted it out loud, the universe was going to come crashing down on her and steal away all her hopes and dreams, and she was never going to be all right again.

If this was a punishment, dangling him in front of her, just to take him away, she wouldn't survive it.

Tristan, the EMT, was Thurstan, her long-lost angel love.

But after this long? She'd never run into someone who looked *exactly* like Thurstan before. She'd also never had the slightest feeling that she might be seeing him just to realize she was wrong. No, she'd *never* had any kind of Thurstan sighting. Men who looked similar enough that she could spend a night with? Sure.

But nothing like this.

Not in four thousand years.

Not unless she'd finally gotten to the point where she was losing her senses.

That could be, but what if it wasn't? What if she

was right, let alone the *how was this possible?* But she'd have to talk to him eventually, right?

Just not yet. Not while he was at the hospital, since he probably wouldn't give her the opportunity to explain anything. He'd just kick her out of these "staff and patients only" areas of the hospital.

That meant following him around like a creeper while she waited for the chance.

He and the other man, Miller, laughed and talked like they were genuinely good friends. Bryony liked that. She liked that Thurstan had companions he found trustworthy.

She liked watching him smile, even if it wasn't for her.

She liked that he appeared healthy, that he had a good job, and people who cared about him.

Even if she did nothing else but watch over him, it was worth it knowing that.

It gave her time to figure out what she'd say to him to convince him he knew her.

I'm going to come off as absolutely delusional if I try to insist to him that we're long-lost lovers.

She thought about appearing at his car after his shift, but she had visions of him immediately calling for backup and a whole squad of hospital staff shoving her into a white jacket while she tried to explain everything.

Could EMTs call for backup like that? Or was

that a police thing? Either way, he appeared hearty, but she didn't want to give him a heart attack either. Or deal with dozens of police and hospital staff showing up and ruining everything.

And *then* she'd have to use her super-human strength to knock everyone away, and she'd have to unfurl her wings and fly away, thus ensuring each of those workers would need her to revisit and mind-wipe them.

At least, that was the excuse she told herself when she failed to talk to him at his car.

So, keeping the invisibility glamor, she took to the air, soaring behind Thurstan as he finished his quiet shift and drove from the hospital, toward the city's residential neighborhoods.

The entire flight, all she could think of was the time they'd spent together in the past.

She couldn't imagine the first time they met because there never was such a time. They were angels, and when the angels were created, they were immediately together. They did not exist, and then they existed—the both of them, together at the same time. Two halves of a whole. Hand in hand, arms around each other, it was how they always were.

She remembered throwing her arms around Thurstan and kissing him.

"But what will I do without you?" Thurstan asked,

feigning a heartbreak by frowning and placing his hand over his chest.

"The same thing you do each time I'm gone." Bryony was dressed in traditional white robes, which she wore when she left him to complete her missions to deliver messages from God to their people.

"Pine for you with each breath and heartbeat until you've returned to me?" he teased, his hands wandering down her back and toward her buttocks.

She laughed and gave him a playful push backward, escaping his grasp. "You will go see our friends and allow them to indulge your brooding while hopefully distracting you away from it."

"Our master should just allow us to go together," Thurstan said, managing to get his arms around her again and nuzzling into her neck. "The message will be seen as stronger if there are two of us, will it not?"

"And if God wanted the message to be stronger, then they would have assigned two to deliver. Besides..." she said, indulging his complaints while preparing to remind him of that which they both already knew.

"I know, I know. I'm not a messenger. I'm a warrior, and I must be here, ready for the day when I'm called to defend God and the heavens by battling all forces of darkness and enemies of our Lord."

It wasn't something they actually thought would happen. There were enough warriors that God rarely sent even half down to fight whenever the occasional uprising did occur, so it was very unlikely Thurstan would be called for anything.

Until the Big One.

The war that changed everything.

How long had they been together before it all ended? Bryony tried to imagine it, but it was impossible to tell. Up in the heavens, time was not measured the same.

But the pain she felt when she lost Thurstan put her on a different existence. Now she knew what every day of four thousand years felt like.

The sun was getting ready to come up over the horizon when he pulled into his apartment complex.

The man looked tired as he emerged from his car. The bags under his eyes made it obvious, as did his slumped shoulders.

Bryony continued to follow him, now on foot, as he walked into the building and up four flights of stairs. She had to assume the elevators must be out. *There is no way a man this tired would still stick to his exercise routine, is there?*

On the sixth—and top—floor, Thurstan sighed and unlocked his door, stopping with the door open while he bent down to pick up the mail, which had been shoved through the slot.

Bryony debated flying over him right then, but she opted to wait rather than risk her wings bumping into anything and further making this man believe that he was being haunted.

When he turned to close the door, she rushed past him, slightly nudging into him.

She only grazed him a little bit, but other than looking around and seeing no one, he shook his tired head and shut and locked the door, probably assuming his stumble was due to fatigue.

He stripped through his bedroom, and pervert that she was, Bryony rushed forward to get a good look. Bryony got a great look at his perfect fucking frame, including the *V* of his hips beneath his clothes as he unbuckled his belt and undid the pants button and zipper. He pushed his pants down, stepping out of them, and Bryony got a good look at his boxer briefs and powerful thighs filling them out.

That wasn't the only part of him that was nicely filled out.

That cock bulge...

Her breath caught.

She shouldn't stare. It was wrong. She was wrong.

He pulled off the boxers, and she got a look at his backside—damn, that ass was sculpted.

Human EMT Thurstan doesn't miss arm, leg, or *ab day,* Bryony mused.

She worked up the willpower to stay outside the bathroom while he showered, giving him some small amount of privacy and hating herself for the lack of boundaries she'd already indulged in.

Bryony took the last few moments she could to prepare herself for their impending confrontation—still unsure what she was going to say.

She couldn't think, however, so she looked around his room instead.

It was so... *mundane*. A simple bed, queen-sized with plain blue sheets, some simple furniture, all in shades of blue and grey. It was all... so human. Regular. Not at all worthy of the magnificent celestial being that Thurstan really was.

Right, because this is Tristan, *not Thurstan,* she reminded herself, starting the whole inner debate all over again.

Thurstan had been an angel warrior, but he was also a healer. A battlefield medic, in a way. And Tristan? An EMT? It made sense, and it wasn't as though living in heaven had required any need for decorating. What would Thurstan have known about wall art or decorative pillows? Bryony certainly didn't know a damn thing about making a space feel welcoming and lived in.

She needed fresh air. This was so fucking overwhelming. Bryony rushed to the far window of his room and opened it, clutching the ledge while taking deep breaths.

She should fly away. She should leave him here, to his life, to his small happiness before she ruined it.

If it wasn't Thurstan, speaking to him would

screw with his head for the rest of his life. Even if she wiped the memory, he could have recurring nightmares of her forever.

If it was Thurstan...

Is this really happening?

For real?

After this long?

Why now?

Is this really possible?

And what could I have possibly done to deserve such a gift if this is true?

She was so overwhelmed and lost in her own panicked thoughts that she didn't pay attention to what was happening in the bathroom—most importantly, when the shower water stopped. It wasn't until the bathroom door opened that she realized she had dropped her glamour and was in full view of Thurstan.

Might as well get it over with.

She spun around, neatly taking a seat on the windowsill, trying to look casual, calm, and collected.

Instead of the mess she actually was.

Even if she might have thought about it for a second.

He stared at her, frozen in place. Was that recognition in his blue eyes?

From when she'd revealed herself to him in the hospital? Or a time before?

"What the..." He looked toward his bedroom door, as if expecting to find some answers there. "What are you doing here?"

Bryony took a breath and smiled.

"We should talk."

Not the way she'd wanted this to happen, but she *needed* to talk to this man. She *needed* to figure out what was going on.

And she wasn't dumb enough to run away from someone who might be the man she'd missed for four thousand years.

FOUR

Tristan toweled off in a daze, brushed his teeth with his head hanging over the sink, and dragged on a pair of mostly clean sweats before he shuffled for the heaven that was his lonely bed.

He stopped short in the doorway of his bedroom, wide fucking awake in an instant, the hairs on the back of his neck standing straight with the feeling that something was different.

Not wrong, but not right either.

He was confused by the fresh breeze that circled through his room. He hadn't left a window—

"What the..." He blinked at the sight of a woman sitting on the windowsill wearing black jeans. She had one foot on the ground in his room, the other pulled up on the ledge, her leather-jacket-covered arms wrapped loosely around it.

The air stirred her wild golden hair that fell in waves past her shoulders, the strands on top shining yellow in the moonlight, while the strands underneath, in shadows, appeared dark enough to be black.

With her back to the rising sun, her face was hidden in shadows, and he couldn't make out the features of her face, but he didn't need to in order to guess what the intruder was there for.

He glanced around. He didn't see anyone outside his room or hear anyone else in his apartment. He must have left the door unlocked.

Great.

"What are you doing here?"

What did robbers want nowadays? It wasn't like he had a stereo for them to steal. Would she accept his earbuds? Probably not, since they were twenty-dollar knockoffs. He didn't own a computer, and his tablet was in his car at the moment.

His television? No, the TV on the wall was probably too large for the woman to carry out on her own.

"We should talk."

He groaned. Did this bitch have a weapon on her? He was too tired for this.

"I have some cash here," he said, breaking the

silence and answering the question he assumed she implied by being there. He went over to the dresser, moving slowly, grabbing up the wadded-up bills.

Mostly small dollars bills, a few fives. "There's a twenty in there somewhere. This is all the cash I got on me."

He'd never been robbed before, and he was too exhausted to want to fight, even if he knew he could take her.

He worked to keep his tone as friendly as he could through the exhaustion. He didn't want her to shoot him if she did happen to be pointing a gun at him.

He stepped closer to her, holding out the bills, before his sleep-desperate brain stopped him.

He shouldn't approach someone who was possibly pointing a weapon at him.

He'd seen too many robberies go wrong because the victim got a little too close.

He tossed the bills on the floor between them.

She could get them herself if that's what she really wanted.

She looked down at the money but didn't move.

"That's not what I came here for."

Jesus Christ.

Okay, so not a robbery? It occurred to him that her posture was far too casual for someone who'd intended to rush in, take stuff, and be gone by the time he was out of the shower.

No, now that he better assessed the situation, he realized it seemed more like she'd been waiting for him.

This suspicion was confirmed when she didn't jump up and snatch the money from off the floor.

She looked more like an invited guest.

Stupid, tired brain, Tristan thought to himself, figuring he must be dreaming or hallucinating a woman again, just like he had back at the hospital.

But the cold night air reminded him that dreams didn't feel real like this. He sighed, trying to think. Maybe one of his neighbor's booty calls had walked into his place accidentally.

She cocked her head to the side, her gold hair falling off her shoulder, her features still hidden in shadow. The light of the moon and stars and yellow street lights behind her cast an ethereal glow behind her.

She seemed to be waiting for something. Waiting for him to do something.

"I'm sorry to let you know, but I think you've come to the wrong place," he said as he went over to turn on the overhead lights, as the morning light still left too much in darkness. The woman hadn't done anything that seemed threatening yet, but he'd still prefer to not be in the dark with a stranger—in his apartment.

He turned back to her, greeted by a stunningly beautiful face. Plump dark lips, perfectly sculpted cheekbones, amber eyes assessing him while he observed her.

She was the face he'd seen in the hospital. The one he'd assumed was an image he'd seen in an advertisement. She was far too beautiful to be real. He shook his head, squeezing his eyes together and re-opening them, hoping the vision would vanish again.

She did not. Instead, she stood, still apparently waiting for him to do or say something. As they neared one another, he saw that though she was tall for a woman, he was still taller. She was muscular though, curvy, but firm. Her body seemed strong, her stance confident. Her dark jeans stopped at her hips, and she wore a white button-down beneath the leather jacket that didn't entirely hide all of her skin, either.

"You don't know me?" she finally asked.

That familiar voice made him jolt.

Thurstan.

He blinked, pushing away that thought and that heavy feeling of *yes, yes, yes,* clawing at the inside of his head.

"No," he answered.

The woman nodded then stepped closer.

He frowned, watching her, the wide heels of her boots thumping across his floor as she came toe to toe with him.

She certainly wasn't afraid of being in a strange place with an unknown man.

"What about now?" She glanced up at him, her pretty amber eyes framed by thick, dark lashes. There was a light dusting of freckles across her nose and cheeks. He hadn't noticed before, but now that she was right here, they were all he could focus on.

And they *did* look familiar.

He lay next to her. Though her eyes were closed, she hadn't been sleeping, just basking in their post-love-making while nestled in his arms. She smiled as he traced his fingers across those familiar dots on her face, creating shapes like he was connecting stars into constellations. Then he dipped down to kiss her lips, and she returned the affection.

As the vision passed through his mind, Tristan's hand automatically reached out, a finger only brushing against her cheek before he snapped out of it and pulled his hand back.

"What is your name?" he asked, forcing himself to step backward.

"Bryony." Her face fell in disappointment, as though she'd wished he already knew—but how could he?

"Got a last name?"

She only smiled sadly at him.

The gesture did something strange to his body. While his stomach wrenched, his chest contracted, and his arms stretched out to her, ready to pull her in for comfort.

She stepped away before he could touch her.

He shook himself out of it. Though he was curious, sleep was clawing at him, and he really didn't have the energy for this.

"Well, Bryony," he said, clearing his throat, "I'm sorry to disappoint, but can I escort you out the way you came?" He gestured toward the front door.

She shook her head slowly.

He sighed and rubbed the bridge of his nose. Maybe he could figure out who she was looking for and then contact that person to come get her. "Who were you expecting to find tonight?"

"No one else," she said, her voice low and throaty. Seductive. Mesmerizing. "Just you."

"Just *mmph*—"

Bryony cut him off by pulling him by the back of his neck with her impossibly strong hands and pressing her lips hard against his.

Something immediately clicked inside his head.

Well, fuck it. A beautiful woman appeared out of nowhere in his room and wanted to get hot and heavy, who was he to turn her away?

Any thought of rejecting her kiss instantly flew out of his mind, while every cell in his body came roaring to life, reacting to *her*—insisting that he pull her into his arms and deepen the embrace. Commanded him to spin her around and lean her into the wall so every inch of him could move against her.

It felt like he'd been given a shot of adrenaline and downed a couple of heavy-duty energy drinks. Sleep was suddenly the last thing on his mind.

The only thing that mattered was the insistence of her lips and her tongue and the strength of her thighs around his waist.

Damn, did she ever know how to kiss.

Definitely wasn't shy about it as she thrust her tongue into his mouth, as if what she found inside would sustain her. Like she needed him to live.

And he couldn't help but feel as if he, himself, had not really been *living* until this moment. He moaned as she thrust her pelvis against him, his cock aching from the friction. She groaned into his mouth, pressing her body more firmly against his.

She pushed off of the wall, feet on the floor again.

"Bed. Now."

He laughed when she pushed him down.

She didn't laugh back. She actually growled at him while shrugging out of her jacket.

"Buy me dinner first, why don't you?" he joked, trying to get ahold of himself.

"Is that what you want?" she asked, her hands stopping on the buttons of her shirt. "Tell me you want me to go, and I'll go."

She almost made it sound like a threat.

He shook his head. "I don't want you to go."

This was strange, in more than one way. If Bryony had seemed befuddled, like she didn't know where she was or where she was supposed to be, he would have insisted on stopping and helping her find out.

But there wasn't a question about the fact that this woman had her eyes set on him. Like he was exactly what she was looking for.

Like they *belonged* together.

Part of him agreed. A big part.

Bryony nodded, shrugging out of her shirt before climbing on top of him, kissed him again. Tristan couldn't hide the reaction his body had at her eager hands sliding across his stomach and chest then shoving down the waist of his sweats, taking a firm hold of his hard cock.

Tristan groaned, his eyes rolling to the back of his head.

It had been so long since he'd had a woman touching him. God it was good. Better still, she moved her hands as though she knew *exactly* how he liked it, one hand firmly at the base, keeping him from coming while her other stroked him from root to tip.

It was only when she dipped her head, her tongue darting out to play along the head of his dick that he found his senses.

Before her lips and tongue touched his cock, he moaned, taking her by the shoulders and gently pushing her back.

"Bryony, wait."

As though him saying her name had stunned her, she allowed him to push her away, blinking widely.

God, he was such an idiot.

"Not that I don't want you to, but you said you came here looking for me. Why?" The sudden thought that this might be an unhinged stalker crossed his mind. Like she might have seen him working at the hospital or bought one of the calendars he was featured in and decided to make a move.

Damn, why'd it have to be that way? All she'd needed to do was introduce herself in a normal setting and he would have absolutely agreed to a proper date.

But if she insisted, he'd fuck her anyway. He wasn't that dumb.

"What does it matter?"

"Because," he said through his teeth, fighting

like hell to be a semi-decent person when his dick throbbed for the touch of her tongue, "this isn't the way I usually go about this."

He looked her in the eyes, squinting to get a better look at the pupils, searching for some hint she might be high on something.

No. Looked normal. He didn't think she was high.

She pushed herself up and tried kissing him again. It was a little slower this time, not quite so eager, but there was something to it that begged for his understanding.

It made his head, both of them, feel all kinds of thick and fuzzy.

She pulled back slowly, her breath heavy, chest heaving, cheeks flushed. "Stop over thinking and just give in."

"What?"

Another kiss. Another sense of softness and righteousness he couldn't ignore.

Once again, she seemed to pull him into a trance, and he was struck with the feeling that he done this with her before. Kissing *this* woman was different than any kiss he'd had before. This felt a little too familiar. Her body against his, her hair in his hands, her lips and her tongue mingling with his.

Fuck, her *tongue*.

His dick throbbed. She thrust against him, mewling softly as he groaned.

He moaned again as she tasted him, dry humping him slow, making every thought in his head about why this was a bad idea sail far, far away.

Tristan couldn't help himself anymore.

So what if she's an admirer who went about this the wrong way? The woman took a shot. It was ballsy, brave, and a little stupid, but whatever.

He could only decline sex with a beautiful woman so many times before *he* was the stupid one.

His hand came up, threading through those thick golden locks, pulling her close.

Giving in.

FIVE

With every step, every movement, Bryony reaffirmed that this *really was Thurstan.*

Under the touch of her hands and mouth, he felt and tasted exactly the same, and yet so, so different.

Thousands of years and being born into a whole new body was likely to do that, but Bryony wasn't complaining as she explored him, kissing his mouth then his neck and shoulders before finally pressing her mouth to his chest and then lower still.

She never in a million years would have thought she would see him again. Yet, here he was, letting her push down his sweatpants again, freeing his cock. She couldn't believe he was wearing something like that—it was a far cry from what they'd worn thousands of years ago.

This man who went by Tristan didn't know her, but he would after tonight, that was for sure.

She was glad he finally stopped trying to put out the flame between them and he allowed her to put her lips around his cock while he stood before her. Bryony took him into her mouth, delighting in the taste of his shaft, which was also familiar. She was pleased when Thurstan shuddered and held on to her shoulder and the back of her head.

Yes. Yes. Yes. She wanted him to touch her. Wanted him to thrust his hips. She'd almost forgotten what this felt like, but now, as she sank her lips around his large dick, pressing him deep inside until he touched the back of her throat, it was as if all those years between them had never happened.

I fucking missed you, Thurstan. Missed you so much.

"Oh, baby," Thurstan moaned, thrusting his cock forward. He was slow about it, gentle in a way he used to be when they were making sweet love but one or both of them was tired.

She reminded herself that though this was her Thurstan, he was human now, and humans didn't have the same energy as Bryony's kind. Plus, paramedics worked long, stressful hours.

That was all right. She would take good care of him.

Finding her rhythm, Bryony bobbed her head, keeping her cheeks hollowed every time she pulled back before slowly sinking down again.

She moved in as far as she could go, opening her throat, trying to hold her position but pulling back when she felt herself choke.

Yeah, he was just as big as he used to be. She was pleased with that. Couldn't wait for him to be inside her again.

She pulled back with a wet popping sound, wiping her mouth with the back of her hand and smiling up at him.

"Scoot up a little. You look like you could stretch out. Relax."

He blinked his wide blue eyes at her, as if her words weren't totally getting through, but then he seemed to understand, and he nodded, pulling her up by her arms with a shocking strength.

"Absolutely."

His voice was hungry, feral, and she could swear she saw the glow of lightning bolts in his eyes when he got into the middle of the bed, taking her with him, kissing her hard.

Bryony felt something inside her cheer when she finally got through to Thurstan's more basic instincts. She wasn't sure if it was because a willing woman was in his arms, eagerly kissing and begging for release, or if it was because *she* was the one in his arms.

She hoped for a little of both.

Thurstan hooked his arm around her middle, turning her over, pinning her to the mattress, and Thurstan's eyes were hungry as he climbed on top of her.

Her legs fell open for him easily. She pressed her hands to his firm shoulders then slid them around his back, up behind his neck, and into his hair when he kissed and sucked on her throat.

She barely managed to toe off her boots. He was already naked, and she was way overdressed.

Thurstan actually growled at her when he pulled back and clumsily helped her out of her clothes.

He opened her button-down, revealing a black sports bra underneath.

So she had worn her working undergarments. How was she to know she'd be running into her millennia-dead ex?

Thurstan didn't care. He peeled the bra off her and moaned at the sight of her breasts, cupping them and squeezing, bringing her pain as well as pleasure as she arched into his touch.

"Don't make me wait," she begged, her black jeans feeling a little too tight as she gyrated against him, her sex hot and throbbing. "I need you—*now*."

Thurstan blinked, his vision seeming a little clearer, and that happy feeling Bryony had suddenly left her when he pulled away from her.

No, no, no. "Where are you—?"

He pulled out a drawer in his nightstand and removed a small item.

"Safety first," he said with a little smile, holding the condom packet between two fingers.

Oh.

Bryony nodded, trying not to think about Thurstan with other people, even though clearly the fact that he had those things on hand meant he had others here before. She used his absence to get her pants off, telling herself it was none of her business how sexually active Thurstan had been while he'd been living in his reincarnated human form.

Besides, she'd indulged in carnal pleasures herself in the years that had passed, even if she'd never loved any of her partners—not like she'd loved Thurstan. So it would be selfish of her to wish he'd been denied the pleasures of the body when he needed it.

Though she appeased herself with the knowledge that he would be getting all his pleasures from *her* from now on.

She smiled at that thought, and his smile widened in return.

Her insides fluttered at the sight.

He always had such a gorgeous smile.

She'd missed it.

But his smile was short-lived as he stared down at her with something akin to being put under a spell. He bit his lip and shook his head slowly, his eyes and hands roaming her body from head to toe and back again.

He came forward. Her legs opened easily for him, and he settled there as surely as though he'd done it a million times before, like that was where his home was.

It was sort of the case, and she relished the feel of him, sliding her hands across the warmth and taut muscles of his chest.

Then he leaned in, pressing his mouth to her breast, his lips tight on her nipple, making Bryony gasp from the sudden shock of pleasure that came with it, and she arched her back, her toes curling, her thighs tightening around his waist.

She fisted the sheets, holding on to them as though they were the last thing tying her to consciousness. The pure ecstasy of her reunion with Thurstan threatened to send her mind into orbit.

"Missed you," she moaned. "So much."

Thurstan's eyes closed as he kissed and sucked on her breast, first one and then the other, and then his heated lips moved on to Bryony's throat.

If he heard what she'd said, he didn't speak of it,

and Bryony was all too happy to let him have her, a smile on her face as he tasted and touched her in a way that she hadn't been touched in millennia.

No one else had come close. She had tried to find someone, but no one's touch lit her on fire the way Thurstan's did.

"You're beautiful," Thurstan said, his voice a low, pleasant rumble against her skin. He kissed and licked and even gently bit her. "You taste so fucking good."

Bryony laughed. "Language."

He didn't often curse in their old life together. She added that to a list of things that had been bound to change after four thousand years. She didn't mind.

She hoped he wouldn't mind the changes in her either.

"Take me," she begged—knowing that was something she *never* did. If Hades and Persephone ever found out she had begged someone like that, even if it was Thurstan, they would never let her live it down. "Please, I *need* you."

She'd waited long enough. She needed their bodies to be fully joined. Fully reunited.

Thurstan pulled back, looking at her as though doubting the situation again.

She swore if he asked if she was sure she was going to lose it.

If he stopped now, Bryony would cry, and she wouldn't give a damn what her underworld friends thought of it. Her body burned with the desperate need for him, and she couldn't wait any longer.

"All right." His voice was gruff, but his hands were quick and sure as he opened the condom packet, tossing it away as he rolled the rubber expertly over his cock.

A cock she couldn't wait to feel inside her.

Bryony's body sang as Thurstan finally settled the thick head of his cock against her sex. No more waiting. She reached down and gripped his hips, desperate to pull him inside her.

No extra asking for the permission she'd already given. Thurstan slid home like it was all he'd been aching for as well.

Bryony opened her mouth with a heavy gasp and then a satisfied sigh as he stretched her, filled her, returned them back to one after so many years apart.

It felt better than she remembered.

Because it was him.

Her legs curled around his waist, her arms around his shoulders, and Bryony buried her face into his neck. "I love you."

He groaned, but again, there was no response, as he just *moved*.

Bryony moaned. There was pain and pleasure, but the good far outweighed the bad. It had been...

an embarrassingly long time since she'd lain with a man, and even the last male she'd bedded hadn't been as big as Thurstan was.

She smiled as he moved inside her. Confidant and familiar as though he could remember doing this before.

Could he? Was this bringing him back? Could he perhaps remember?

Is that even possible for a human mind? She didn't want to think about the possibility that he wasn't capable of regaining his memories.

"Oh!" Bryony's head fell back into his sheets as his quick pace became unbearably fast. Their flesh slammed together hard, making sticky, slapping sounds between them that Bryony absolutely loved.

"Harder," she begged, thrusting her hips to meet his, clenching her walls around his cock and loving the way he groaned and closed his eyes. "Fuck me harder. I *need* you."

She needed him like she needed air to breathe. She wanted to feel him long after this was done because she didn't want to mistake it for a dream.

She needed him like she needed her wings. Like she needed her eyes to see, and now that she had him again, for the life of her, Bryony did not understand how she'd managed so long without him.

He growled at her, grabbing her by her wrists

and pulling them up above her head, stretching her torso out for him and putting her breasts on even more of a display than they already were.

She smiled up at him, enjoying his roughness, knowing he wouldn't take it much further than this. He liked to dominate her, and she enjoyed his efforts, but even in his angel form, he'd been too gentle a soul to do much more than this.

"Is that... the best you have?" she teased, the same way she did in the past when she wanted to challenge him, push his limits just a little further each time.

His blue eyes flew wide, and for two long seconds, it looked as though she'd somehow managed to break him out of his trance.

Then, no, Thurstan snarled at her again, his grip tightening, and Bryony even made a play to pretend to try to escape, even though she didn't want to, knowing he would enjoy it.

He did.

"Be still, woman," he commanded, with the exact words and the exact tone he'd used before.

Bryony shivered as he moved his hips again, fucking into her and making Bryony sing her allegiance to him.

"*Yes*," she moaned. "Yes, I will."

Only for you.

He leaned in, kissing her hard on her mouth, his lips claiming authority over her, quieting her words while enticing her to give more of herself to him.

Bryony didn't care. She only wanted to keep up. She wanted the pleasure. She wanted *him*.

And it was coming to a climax too soon as she felt her orgasm building.

"I'm almost there," she cried out. "Come with me. I need us to come together."

He groaned, one hand releasing her wrist so he could slide his palm down her arm, over her shoulder and neck, then cupping her breast.

It left her one arm free to do the same, touching him everywhere she could while her other arm remained trapped under his intense grip.

Of course, she knew that if she chose to move, she was strong enough to get out of his human grasp, but she wouldn't need to. He would release her.

He always did. She trusted him beyond all others, and though he might not know it, he at least seemed to sense it.

His grip lessened on her wrist, his palm sliding up to intertwine his fingers with hers, holding tightly as their bodies thrusted and moved together.

Bryony couldn't hold it back any longer. Thurstan had taken her to the precipice, and her body couldn't slow down. She sailed over it, her entire body convulsing with an orgasm strong enough to shatter the earth.

She threw her head back, moaning, crying out, as the intensity was too much for her to handle and Thurstan fucked her through it.

As the most intense ones subsided, Thurstan reached his climax, gasping and grunting while his body moved in a few final short thrusts.

Then, they lay still, staring into each other's eyes while their bodies still vibrated against each other and Bryony's channel grasped and released him until he finally collapsed on top of her.

He didn't usually do that. Normally he would fall to the side or back, allowing her to cuddle onto him, depending on their position.

He was heavy, but she wasn't about to tell him that. Besides, she didn't mind in the least.

He was like an oversized blanket, shielding her from the rest of the world, and as Bryony breathed through the pleasant humming of her pleasure, she realized how bright it suddenly was in his bedroom.

The sun was not fully up, but it was now in the full process of waking, casting long shadows with golden light.

Dawn always felt so sweet after a long battle, and Bryony realized she'd waited for this particular dawn ever since the day he was taken from her.

"What... what did you do to me?" Thurstan

groaned, finally rolling off of her and taking a deep breath.

Bryony could not respond. She pressed her lips together, fighting against the burning in her eyes. It was all so much. She never thought she'd see him again.

Even so, she would not become some weepy maiden in front of him, especially not after such wonderful lovemaking.

"Thurstan, I—"

A soft snore interrupted her before she could finish.

Bryony blinked, propping herself up on an elbow so she could look down at him.

Sure enough, his eyes were closed. He was fully asleep.

She laughed, the ridiculousness of it chasing away any tears that had been threatening to fall.

She kissed his face instead.

"You always did need your rest after making love to me."

The fact that he still needed it was endearing to her, but she also knew it had something to do with his human body needing rest from a long day of work.

She'd let him sleep. She was sure he needed it. When he woke, he would likely have many questions, and Bryony would need to fill in the gaps for him.

Perhaps she should rest, too—to prepare herself for what was surely to be an intense conversation.

SIX

Tristan opened his eyes and could immediately tell it was just past noon.

He never slept that long, even when he tried. Something inside him always woke up by ten or eleven in the morning at the latest.

He glanced to the side at the clock on his nightstand.

Almost two thirty.

Jesus Christ, how did he manage to—

Oh. He understood now. His guest from the night before was still here, snuggled securely against him, her cheek pressing against his chest, arm around his waist, as though preventing him from going anywhere.

Her naked breasts pressed against his side while

her thigh had moved up and over his, as though holding on to him in a full-body snuggle.

His limbs still felt heavy, his body... sated from what they'd done the night before.

He'd thought perhaps it was a dream, but the gorgeous blonde was snuggled beneath him, curled up like he was her own personal blanket.

And he had been wrapped around her like he couldn't bear to let her go, yet he had to. He carefully untangled himself and slid from the bed.

What the fuck did I do last night?

Not that he was complaining. She was a pretty face to open his eyes to. A nice welcome to the lonely nothing he'd had every morning for the last little while.

She mumbled something incoherent and rubbed her face into his sheets, getting comfortable again and settling down in the space Tristan had vacated.

Soft skin, bright blonde hair, and he could remember how rough he'd been the night before. There were bruises on her wrists. Holy shit.

He grabbed his pants, dressing quickly. He didn't have a shift that night, which was good. It gave him time to figure this out.

Who was she? Where did she come from? How did she get into his apartment? Why was she sitting on the windowsill waiting for him? He vaguely remembered using a condom, and he was grateful for that much.

"Good morning."

Tristan paused, T-shirt in hand as he slowly turned.

The golden-haired woman looked like his every teenage fantasy come to life as she lay on his bed, hair splayed out behind her, breasts gently rising and falling as she breathed, and a welcoming smile on her face.

His dick twitched in response to her, and as much as he wouldn't mind going back to bed for another round with her, he needed to understand the situation now that he was rested and thinking clearly.

First thing's first.

"Good morning—or rather, afternoon." He smiled. "Want something to eat?"

"Just you." She crooked her finger, beckoning him forward.

His stomach had been rumbling, and he had so many questions, but she looked so damned good that his need for sustenance and answers subsided. Like a dog on a leash, he came when he was called.

She pushed herself to her knees when he got onto the bed, and with a shocking strength, she shoved him down, her fingertips trailing down his chest and stomach before her lips and tongue did the same.

"I let you have your sleep, but it was torture waiting." She inched down, down, down, and by the time her slender fingers curled around his cock, he was aching, his dick throbbing, and he moaned when she took him into her mouth.

Was he absolutely sure he wasn't dreaming this?

Tristan covertly pinched himself, making sure she didn't see it.

Nope. This was definitely real, and he let himself relax and enjoy it.

As far as waking up went, this was one of the better ways to do it. He wasn't about to complain.

The more he relaxed, the more memories flowed back to him—from last night and... from something else.

Bryony. That was her name. She told it to him last night, but the name wasn't unfamiliar to him, even though he'd never met someone with that name before.

"Bryony," he groaned, testing her name to be sure, pushing his fingers through her hair.

She glanced up at him, her shocked expression melting into something pleased. As if she was preening at the sound of her name on his tongue.

Then she put her tongue back to good use.

He moaned and enjoyed himself, and damn, if

Bryony wasn't skilled at what she did.

The orgasm she gave him was sudden and left him reeling, left him thinking—and feeling—things that were *way* too serious, considering he didn't know anything about this woman.

Not that he had to share those thoughts and feelings with her. Anyone worth their salt knew that proclaiming love for a partner after one, or even two, amazing orgasms was a surefire way to ruin any chances for... well, anything.

The least he could do was take her on a proper date and let her get to know him before she decided to run.

When she settled back on the bed, looking pleased as punch for having brought him to climax, he immediately slid down to his knees, grabbing her legs and pulling her to the edge of the bed.

She let out a shocked little yell at having her whole body maneuvered like that, her pink, puffy lips wide in an eager smile.

Tristan pushed her legs apart and leaned in for a deep, open-mouthed kiss on her sex. He gave her as good as she dished out.

He left Bryony a quivering, gasping mess when he finished with her, and the dazed way she stared up at the ceiling when he pulled away, along with her chest heaving for breath, left him feeling all kinds of proud.

He wasn't done. He needed to take care of her.

"So, do you like waffles?" he asked.

"Waffles?" She laughed, locking her beautiful amber eyes with his and hitting him with a smile that lit him up inside.

"Or whatever you prefer, if you were up for sticking around, that is."

Just last night he was trying to find any way to convince this stranger to leave his apartment, and now here he was, hoping she'd stay.

Because she should stay. She belongs here. The thoughts floated through his mind, but he tried to push them away. He wasn't the kind of man who fell for someone so easily. What was it about this woman that was making his own thoughts and feelings seem foreign to him?

She eyed him, her head tilting just a little as she reached her hand out, touching his face.

A shockingly gentle act from a stranger.

"What do you remember?"

Not usually the best question to open with.

"Not gonna lie, not a whole lot."

"About us?"

"I'm sorry, but yeah," he said. "Do you work at a hospital or something? I would think I'd remember a name like Bryony, not to mention someone who looks like"—he gestured up and down at her still naked and flushed body—"you."

Bryony's expression twisted to something more akin to hurt. He didn't like putting that look on her face, but now that they were broaching the topic, there was no turning back. He had to be honest with her, help her understand that the admiration had been one-sided—at least before last night.

He turned from her, snagging his discarded clothes and dressing again.

When he turned back, Bryony had grabbed one of his pillows. She sat cross-legged, putting the pillow over her lap and chest, covering herself and holding on to it like it was her lifeline.

"You don't remember me? But I thought... after last night..."

Shit. He'd really hoped she'd be cool about this, but it seemed more and more like there was a misunderstanding here. Maybe she really did think he was someone else, in which case, he should have never let himself indulge.

Damn it!

"I'm sorry," he said. "Look, if I... I didn't mean to lead you on. You seem to think we have a history together, but..." He sighed. How did you try to get someone to understand that, at best, they're confusing you with someone else?

Suddenly, Bryony reached out, taking his hand in her steely grip. "Thurstan, you must remember *some* things. The way you—"

"Tristan."

She blinked. "Come again?"

"My name is *Tristan*," he said, taking a breath. Okay. So this could be good. Well, not good that he slept with a woman while she thought she was with someone else but good in the sense that she wasn't mentally ill. "You're thinking I'm someone else. Did you meet this Thurstan guy in a chat room or—"

She shook her head quickly. "No. I met you."

Fuck. "No, it's not me." Tristan began pacing, one hand on his hip, the other gesturing, as he would if he were working out a complex math equation in the air. "You think I'm someone else."

"No, I—" A banging on his apartment door stopped whatever she had been about to say.

They went from looking at each other to now staring down the hall toward the door.

That wasn't a knock. It sounded like someone had been trying to get in.

"I'm not expecting anyone, are you?" Tristan asked, his voice low. "I mean, is there someone out there looking for you? Who knows you've come here?"

A jealous boyfriend, maybe? Perhaps the man named 'Thurstan she'd been looking for.

"No." Bryony was already pushing herself out of his bed, pulling on her clothes, her eyes glued to his door as though waiting for it to get kicked in but not in a way that suggested she had an idea of who was on the other side.

He didn't know if he should believe her or not because she looked like she was getting ready to attack. Or defend.

Another banging. Tristan could see the way his door curled inward, pulling against the lock and the hinges, like an oversized heartbeat. The drywall on either side of it cracked.

Someone was definitely trying to get in here.

Maybe Bryony had locked the door after herself when sneaking in here last night. Whatever happened, he was glad for it because it was buying them a few more seconds.

"Stay back," he said, lunging to his dresser and retrieving the handgun he kept in the back of the top drawer. He checked the chamber first before sliding in a fully loaded magazine.

Bryony frowned. "What's that for?"

Was she serious?

He pointed at the door with his free hand like it should have been obvious, but she still seemed confused.

Did she expect him to deal with whatever the fuck was on the other side of his door *without* a weapon?

"Just stay right here. Get dressed. I'll deal with this."

CHAPTER

SEVEN

Thurstan was really about to try to stand his ground against Lucifer himself with nothing more than a handgun.

Bryony knew exactly who was on the other side of the door. How he'd found her, that was another question.

What he wanted?

She didn't care to wait around and find out.

"I have a better idea," Bryony said, grabbing Thurstan's arm. "How about we go to my favorite breakfast spot?"

He looked at her as though she were insane, and she could understand why. But before he tried to explain to her how he had other priorities at the moment, she pulled them both out of there.

Through the portal she used to go back and forth between Earth and the Underworld.

When they stepped out into her apartment, Thurstan gasped for breath and shivered, his human body reacting better to a first portal than she might have expected him to.

"What the fuck just happened?" he wheezed, steadying himself on her couch. The gun dropping uselessly from his hand to the floor. "Where are we?"

"Uh, welcome to my place," she offered meekly, taking his human weapon, holding the handle with two pinched fingers, and setting it aside.

His wide eyes conveyed the fact that he wasn't amused and expected more elaboration. Then he focused on her, and she knew he was taking in her true form. Her glamor didn't hold through the portal, so her horns and wings were prominently on display.

"I can put them away," she said, quickly reactivating the glamour, though she didn't usually apply it in the Underworld. Then she gulped, taking a breath and sitting on the couch before she started speaking again. "So, yeah. We're in the Underworld."

She could see the whites all around Thurstan's wide eyes.

"Hell?"

She nodded. "Yeah."

"Like with the devil and stuff?"

"Lucifer lives in another part of the Underworld that's known as Hell. Lucifer isn't in this section. He was back at your apartment though."

"*What?*"

She took a deep breath. This wasn't getting any easier. She may as well just keep speaking the truth.

"Yeah. Lucifer. I don't know how he found you— or me—or why he was there, but likely it wasn't good, so I figured it was best to get out of there."

He sat on the couch, holding his head. "I'm losing my mind. I hallucinated voices and faces and then a whole woman and amazing sex and now Lucifer and the Underworld?"

"You aren't hallucinating anything. This is all real."

"What the hell does Lucifer want with me? Why was he at my place?"

She shrugged. "The same thing Lucifer wants from anyone. Their soul. Their pledge to be loyal servants to him."

"Well *why now,* then? Why after you show up..." he trailed off, giving her an accusatory look.

"Yeah, I probably led him to you, though I had no idea he was following me. Look, Thurstan—"

"*Tristan!*" he snapped, looking at her. "Stop calling me *Thurstan.*"

"I can't. Because you *are* Thurstan. I don't know how this is possible, but it is. As hard as it is for me to wrap my own mind around, I've seen nothing but proof that it's true. Up to and including Lucifer showing up at your place."

"And who *is* Thurstan, then?"

Here it was. Time to say it out loud.

"Thurstan is the man I loved. The other half of me. He... died... four thousand years ago."

Thurstan's face went from shock to disbelief quickly. He stood and paced her living room, rubbing his temples and chanting under his breath, "There's no place like home, there's no place like home."

"You're not going to wake up from a dream like Dorothy," Bryony said.

"Whatever, I'm still trying it."

That got her right in the chest.

Suck it up. She could do this.

"I'm starving. How about we stop talking about this for a bit and go get something to eat?"

She glanced down at herself.

Maybe she should get some clothes on.

"What about Lucifer?" he snapped. "Is he breaking into my place right now, or did he just follow us down here?"

"He probably left your place when we did, sensing we were gone. He's not here, because this isn't his territory and he's restricted from portaling in."

Bryony stood. "Wait right here."

She went to her room.

She wanted to wear something nice. She wanted to look good for him, but she didn't want to leave Thurstan alone for long either.

Luckily, Bryony was used to picking out good outfits and shoes in record time. She washed her face, applied a touch of lipstick, and was ready to go in less than five minutes.

Thurstan was standing right where she'd left him, looking shellshocked and not entirely there.

Bryony sighed. "Right, shall we?"

She headed to the front door, gesturing for Thurstan to follow.

To her relief, he did.

And he stopped asking questions long enough for them to portal to her favorite diner and get seated at the table by the window she liked best.

Thurstan twisted his body and head this way and that, trying to take everything in again.

Two portals in less than ten minutes apart from each other. That had to be rough.

She nudged a menu his way. He didn't look at it.

He kept looking around, eyeing the other patrons before whispering, "Can we keep talking about stuff in here?"

The chatter in the diner was calm. The windows bright and open, porcelain clinking softly together, the sun pouring in, and the smell of coffee lingering in the air as the gentle breeze ruffled through the many hanging ferns.

It probably looked to him like a normal cafe.

"I don't see why not," she replied. "Everyone here is like us."

"Us?"

"Not quite human."

He nodded, and she assessed that it wasn't that he understood completely but that he wasn't ready to revisit the topic of what he might be.

Maybe he thought she misspoke.

The waitress came by and took their order.

"Waffles for me, please," Bryony said, remembering that was what Thurstan wanted to feed her. "With bacon, coffee, and orange juice."

"Of course, and for you, sir?"

"Oh, uh..." He looked at Bryony helplessly, as if he were being asked to answer the meaning of the universe.

She let him work it out on his own. "The, uh, same? Please?"

His smile was all nerves and plastic as he handed the waitress the menu. She took it with a cheery smile. "First time here? Don't worry, we'll take good care of you."

Thurstan immediately went pale.

Bryony struggled not to laugh at him.

"Why does this place look so much like... the, uh,

not Underworld? I mean, everything has kind of a blue tinge, but the buildings all look normal," Thurstan said after the waitress left.

"There are differences, but mostly the Underworld was built up with influences from Earth architects. The living and the departed," she said. "And don't worry. The waitress didn't mean anything by it. She was talking about the service."

"Right." He looked around suspiciously. "Is everyone here... evil?"

"No." Bryony shook her head, laughing a little. "This is a neutral area. Folks of all sorts live here with no good or evil intentions toward each other."

Thurstan frowned, like he didn't get it. "Have you always lived here? Are you a demon?"

"No. I was an angel, but after I left heaven, I joined a few other refugees in the Underworld."

"You... you're a fallen angel?"

"Not exactly," she replied. "Usually that term is reserved for those who sided with Lucifer and stood against God. Though I guess those in heaven would consider me fallen, since refusing to serve the Lord is in essence standing against him."

She shrugged and gratefully took the cup of coffee the waitress brought by, swallowing it down hot and black and then accepting a refill that the waitress had ready. *Ahhh, sweet nectar.*

The magic beans—as popular in the Underworld

as they were on Earth—gave her the extra push she needed to return to the topic at hand while the cooks prepared their breakfast.

"I'm going to lay it all out there for you. I suppose I should have yesterday before we were intimate, but honestly, after four thousand years of missing someone, can anyone really blame me that I was more focused on a physical reunion?"

"Right, four thousand years." For whatever reason, Thurstan was following along the story now, no longer fighting the truths she shared or even acting shocked about it.

"You are the reincarnated human form of my angel partner, Thurstan. You *are* Thurstan. You're just... human. And missing his memories."

"Yep, you kind of explained that before. Wait, Thurstan was an angel? Like you were?"

"I still am," she said, feeling a little defensive and needing to clear that up. "Well, as far as having the same powers I had as an angel."

"But you don't call yourself an angel?"

"I'm a fury now, technically," she replied. "An angel in nature, but a vigilante in practice."

He nodded again, seemingly still focused on just accepting what she had to say. Then the statement seemed to process.

"A vigilante?"

She nodded.

She could almost see the cogs whirring in his brain. "I saw you yesterday at the hospital."

She took another drink of coffee, letting him work it out. "You did."

Another brief silence. He stared at her for a long time. "Are you the one who fucked up that guy Billy yesterday?"

She probably shouldn't have smiled so proudly. "Yeah, that was my work."

And she *was* proud that she'd done it. Proud and not a bit regretful, even if she feared Thurstan's reaction to it.

He paused then chuckled a little, reaching for his own coffee and smiling back at her. "Good. That's... you know what? I'm glad. He deserved it."

And the old Thurstan wouldn't have smiled proudly back at her. This one did, and it lit her up from the inside out.

I suppose we're both a little different now than we were so long ago.

The server brought their food, and they ate for a while.

Thurstan eyed his waffles with some suspicion, watching as Bryony smothered her own with butter and syrup before he let himself take a bite.

He moaned, his blue eyes sliding shut. "Oh my God,"

"Good, right?" Bryony said. She'd always

wanted to bring him here. This place came into being long after he'd died. She was so happy he could enjoy it now. "Just don't invoke *you know who's* name too much here. It's supposed to be a neutral space."

"Right, right," Thurstan said, his mouth full as he dug in.

They ate quietly for a little while.

That was always a sign of a good eatery. When the patrons were quietly enjoying their delicious meals.

Finally, Thurstan shared his thoughts with her.

"I'll admit I've had strange feelings of belonging with you, but when that happens, it's almost like I go into a trance-like state. It would be easier to believe that you're some kind of witch putting these strange thoughts in my mind. I mean if I'm going to believe in the supernatural in general, why not just assume that you're playing some kind of trick on me?"

"You can believe anything you want." Bryony sighed, reaching for her fourth coffee refill. "From the moment I saw you, I've been hoping for you to remember, but it didn't happen when I called out to you. It didn't happen when I showed myself—"

"I am so glad I wasn't hallucinating that," Thurstan grumbled. "I thought I was going crazy."

"Yeah, sorry about that." Bryony cringed.

"Maybe next time I see someone I know to be dead I'll be better about approaching them."

He laughed. "So you were hoping that hearing or seeing you would spark my memory, but that failed."

"And sex failed." She drowned the rest of her coffee, hoping for some sort of relief to wash away the crippling disappointment.

Before she could start strategizing other ways to try to get Thurstan's memory back, a couple entered the diner, pulling everyone's attention toward them.

The gentle chatter stopped. The sounds of forks on plates went silent. Everything was still.

Even Thurstan took a look, forcing Bryony's attention as well.

"Shit," she muttered.

"What?"

Hades wore black jeans and a pressed purple button-up. His black hair was slicked back, and he had a small diamond skull pinned to his shirt.

Persephone stood next to him, her arm wrapped around his, his white-gloved hands holding her gently. She was as beautiful as ever in her soft pink dress that reached down to her sandalled feet, her long red hair floating around her. Real spring flowers bloomed in the gentle red waves.

"Who's that?" Thurstan asked. "They look important... Is... is that Lucifer?"

"No, it's just Hades and Persephone." Bryony

shrugged. She hadn't meant to see them yet, but she supposed it wasn't the worst timing in the world.

They spotted her. Bryony raised a hand to wave them over since she *knew* there would be questions. "They're friends of mine and are kind of like the host and hostess of the Underworld. The non-Lucifer parts, anyway."

"Lucifer and Hades are two different people?"

She didn't have time to explain it to him. She rose and gave both her friends hugs, starting with Persephone, who, as always, smelled of fresh flowers.

Hade's hug was as stiff as ever, but he only hugged her because his darling Persephone insisted on it.

Which was why Bryony always held on to him a few second too long and a little too tight, knowing he didn't like it.

"It's so good to see you," Persephone said.

"You as well," Bryony replied, releasing Hades only when he growled a little at her. She switched sides to sit next to Thurstan, allow Persephone and Hades room in their booth.

"Coincidence, you showing up here this morning," Bryony commented, knowing it certainly wasn't one at all.

"No coincidence," Hades replied dryly, straightening his shirt and adjusting his now crooked pin.

"The gossip network here is *incredibly* swift. I heard a strange face had appeared in town and wanted to meet you myself."

"He's not a strange face," Persephone said, her voice dreamy as she looked from Tristan to Bryony. "He's your lost love, is he not?"

Hades and Persephone had never met Thurstan, but Bryony knew Persephone had a way of knowing things. Knowing romantic things, especially.

A gift only the woman who'd fallen in love with Hades himself could possess.

Bryony nodded, feeling a new warmth rising within herself.

If Persephone herself picked up on it, then it was definitely true.

More and more evidence piled in. Bryony loved it. "Yes, Hades, Persephone, meet Thurstan."

"Tristan," he corrected, wiping his hands and leaning over the table to shake Hades' and Persephone's hands.

Bryony's eye twitched. Was she going to have to start thinking of him with the new name, or would he eventually come around to going back to his old one?

"It's so good to meet you," Persephone said, sounding, as always, like she'd woken up on the right side of the bed. "I was so happy to hear you might be back."

"Back, right."

"I don't want you to think we're intruding," Persephone said quickly. "I know this must be a lot, so, well, I won't say much else. That's for you and Bryony, but I just want you both to know how happy we are for you that you're getting this chance."

Bryony wasn't so sure Persephone's words were having the impact she thought they were. Even as Bryony looked at him, all this talk of being back and second chances probably sounded so...so *clingy* and over the top to him.

But looking at his face, she couldn't tell what he was thinking whether he thought this was too much and couldn't wait to get out of here or if he was genuinely interested in learning more about this supposed past life of his.

Thurstan asked more questions. He steered away from any questions about Persephone and Hades specifically. They held hands on top of the table. It was clear to anyone who looked they were deeply in love, and Hades was well known for his devotion to her.

But the way their relationship had started had been the subject of some serious gossip for a long time.

Much of it was true.

But so much of it was not.

Hades got a little sensitive whenever it was

brought up, so Bryony was glad to see the two men at ease around each other.

Suddenly, and without warning, another old familiar face appeared, standing next to their table. Tall and cold.

Hades growled, his gloved hand reaching back as he angled his body, shielding Persephone.

Bryony recognized her instantly. Despite how thin she now was. Despite her golden hair shaved off. Despite the scar that ran down her now crooked nose and lips.

They hadn't seen each other since the war.

"Terry," she greeted, knowing why the fallen angel was there.

Unlike Bryony, Terry hadn't chosen to simply not serve.

She'd chosen a side.

She was once a messenger angel for God, like Bryony, but then joined Lucifer's side in the war.

After what happened to Thurstan, Bryony never fully forgave her.

"Lucifer demands an audience," Terry said, handing over a letter with a recognizable wax seal, not showing any recognition or warmth toward Bryony, which Bryony expected. Lucifer's fallen angels were a bit dim, after being brainwashed for so long by the dark lord.

It wasn't entirely Terry's fault.

But yet, somehow it also completely was.

"Can we have a moment?" Bryony asked

The messenger nodded curtly and left, waiting for them at the front doors of the restaurant.

As if guarding the door to make sure they wouldn't run.

Bryony was furious.

Bryony broke the seal to the letter and read it.

Bryony and Thurstan,

There's no point in running forever. Come to me now and let's get this over with.

~ Lucifer

She tossed the letter on the table so the others could read it.

Persephone's expression fell at the sight of it.

Hades' lips thinned before he set the letter back on the table.

"Well, on that note, I'm taking my beloved back home," Hades announced, standing from the booth, determined as always to stay away from Lucifer's business and remain neutral. He caught the waitress's eye. "This table is on my tab."

"Hades," Bryony started.

"No arguments," he responded curtly.

"It was nice to meet you," Persephone said to Thurstan before giving Bryony a small hug, squeezing her shoulder. "Good luck. I know you will do well."

"Do we have any other choice but to go with Terry?" Thurstan asked when the others left. "Will she fight us if we try to leave?"

"Terry is a messenger angel, not a warrior, like you," she added, still hoping that anything might provoke his memory. "She won't fight us, but Lucifer will keep coming after us. He'll keep sending messenger angels until he sends warrior ones, who I don't think—even buff as you are—you can win against."

"And if I go back to my place, then he's going to bust my door down," Thurstan correctly assessed. "Well, at least this way I don't need to replace any doors or windows or broken furniture, right?"

She smiled softly. "You're always looking at the brighter side of things."

EIGHT

"I thought you said they couldn't get in this section," Thurstan said as they left their table and headed to the door, without paying, since Hades was, apparently, a nice enough guy that he bought people breakfast.

"I said Lucifer can't come here. The fallen angels can, so he can send messengers in for him."

Terry barely nodded at them and turned. She waved her hand in front of the door before opening it.

They all stepped through the restaurant door, but instead of stepping out onto the sidewalk, the same one they'd used when they'd gone to the restaurant, they stepped out into a whole other area.

Instead of a city street, they were in a desolate courtyard, outside of a gothic castle, surrounded by what looked like a medieval city—or what Tristan thought must be one—with all the little houses made of planks or stone with thatched roofs.

And there was definitely a red haze in the air and sky, unlike the blue they'd left behind in Hade's area, with a thin haze of fog that went right to his bones.

He sucked in a breath. "I'm never going to get used to that."

"Portals can feel different depending on where they go," Bryony explained. "Welcome to Hell."

"Very different from where we just were." Tristan shuddered. "No modern-day architectural influences like the neutral zone?"

"Lucifer can go up to Earth—he's powerful enough to—but his fallen angels can't," Bryony answered, speaking loud enough for Terry to hear, though she didn't indicate if she was even listening.

"Looks like the last time they got any inspiration for their buildings was about five hundred years ago. In Transylvania."

Bryony smiled. "Pretty much. Lucifer is, well, Lucifer. He loves all the creepy shit. Bats and wolves and dead trees. Fallen angels have been here since the day they lost the war, and if they venture to Earth, they risk being attacked by God's warrior angels."

"But they can go to the Underworld. Wouldn't that influence the architecture?"

"They *can* be sent to the Underworld on a task from Lucifer," Bryony clarified. "But he doesn't allow them trips over there for fun. He doesn't want to chance giving them any freedom, any chance to interact with others. Though if they cared to talk to insiders, I'm sure they'd tell us that they just preferred to stay amongst themselves."

"So this is a cult?"

Bryony laughed. "Basically."

"Let's go." Terry motioned her shaved head toward the castle. Bryony and Tristan followed.

He wasn't sure if he should be nervous. He got a sense of safety standing next to Bryony—an angel... a real angel!—but he was nervous all the same.

Meeting Lucifer? The biggest, baddest demon in all human lore? A couple of hours ago, he wasn't so sure he believed in that stuff, and now he was going to meet the guy. It didn't seem to be something he should be relaxed about, though Bryony's face was certainly stoic.

As if this was an everyday thing for her.

Was she afraid? Or was she putting on a brave face?

He wished he knew. He wished he knew anything about her, actually.

Ever since she'd told him they had a history—a past life—together, he'd been frustrated that if it were true, he had no connection to it.

Well, not *no* connection. He certainly felt a pull toward Bryony that could be described as nothing less than otherworldly.

Too bad that instead of exploring that pull, they had to have an audience with the devil.

They walked through the courtyard and right to Lucifer's castle. Terry guided them toward the gatehouse.

Tristan searched around, looking for any signs of people guarding the entrance. Demons. Monsters. Anything with horns and scales and fangs.

He looked at Bryony.

"Why the wings and horns on both good and evil?" he asked, nodding from Terry to Bryony. He should have been more unsettled by seeing Bryony with her wings and horns, but it actually didn't bother him. He thought it should have, but on her, it seemed normal.

Fitting.

She looked beautiful, ethereal, and absolutely perfect to him.

"I thought it was supposed to be white wings for angels, horns and forked tails for devils?"

"We both have both," Bryony answered with a little smile, as if she thought his line of questioning was amusing. "I think the lore says that... what? Fallen angels get their wings stripped and get horns and tails instead? That doesn't happen. Our bodies and powers didn't change when we left the heavens. We were always like this. The wings and tail are the part of us that reflect our master's true nature."

"Huh?" Tristan didn't follow.

"God's dragon form." She glanced at him and saw how confused he was. "Ah, right. You probably didn't learn that, since that piece isn't in everyday God lore anymore. See, God's natural form is a dragon. They created the humans, and their highest angels can shift into dragon *or* human form. The rest of us are a combination of both. Human form with dragon wings and dragon horns."

"Dragons don't have feathery wings," Tristan objected.

"You've seen a dragon?" Bryony asked.

"Well, no," he admitted. "But really? No tail?"

"You better stop looking at Terry's ass." Bryony elbowed him but gave a small laugh to let him know she wasn't actually mad.

"I want to look at no one's ass but yours," Tristan said without thinking, nearly growling in Bryony's ear.

He shocked himself because he meant it. With everything inside him, he meant it, and the look of shock and pleasure she gave made him wish they were back in his bedroom before any of these revelations had come to light.

Terry guided them through a long stone corridor.

Their footsteps echoed. Ratty tapestries hung by threads along the wall, damp and old and falling apart.

The hall opened through a double doorway like a wide mouth into a great hall, where Tristan nearly dropped on sight as his eyes locked onto a giant red and black creature sitting leisurely on a tall throne.

"That..." He swallowed hard. "That dragon doesn't have feathers," was all he managed to say, barely keeping the tremble out of his voice.

The creature rested a wide, square face against a red fist, its massive, hooked claws around the size of his thigh. The curved horns were longer than his whole height and ended in massive points, which had probably impaled many men over the years.

"Yeah, Lucifer burned them off," Bryony explained quietly, though her voice still seemed to carry in the large space. She folded her hands in front of her and stopped a few feet from the monster, still seeming unbothered by him.

Tristan, on the other hand, was very well aware that perhaps staying in the Underworld forever with this beautiful, mysterious woman might have been preferable to getting eaten by a dragon. He was starting to think Bryony's laissez-faire attitude wasn't a sign she could protect herself here.

Rather it was indicative of the fact that if Lucifer

wanted to destroy her, he could, and there was nothing she could do about it.

And she knew it.

We should've talked a little more about walking into this pit.

Did they need Terry to portal them out of there, or could Bryony do it? Tristan looked for Terry. He hadn't noticed when she left, but the bald woman was nowhere to be seen, and he was alone with Bryony and... *the devil.*

The dragon's big yellow eyes were fixed on them. Then, suddenly, in a blink of an eye, the dragon was gone, and in its place was a seemingly mundane human man.

Tall and thin, looking to be in his mid-to-late forties with black hair and a soul patch on his pointy chin. The man wore a fully black suit—pants, jacket and button-up shirt—except for the bright red tie.

Tristan was taller than he was, and despite knowing who he was, what he was capable of, Tristan felt calmer seeing him like this.

This guy looked like he got his head shoved into toilets in high school.

Tristan's eyes lingered on the gold pin over his left breast pocket. It reminded him of the skull pin Hades wore. It was in the shape of wings, and he realized that it could be dragon wings or devil wings

—perhaps they were exactly the same. It was something he'd never considered before.

Not that he'd ever had to consider such a thing

"Well, well," the man said, nodding at Bryony and then smiling in a way that looked like he'd caught them in the middle of something. "How are you, sweet Bryony? It's been a long time."

"What the fuck do you want, Lucifer?" Bryony growled. "I'm busy."

Tristan blinked. This was bad. He could deal with the fact that she was an angel—or fury, whatever—who lived in the Underworld and beat up human criminals for fun, but he couldn't protect her if she mouthed off to Satan.

"Uh, hey there," Tristan said quickly, stepping in front of Bryony and ignoring her shock, and outraged, expression. "I'm not sure what you wanted to see us for, sir, but, well, we're here. So... what's up?"

"Thurstan." She grabbed his shoulder.

He shrugged her off, not taking his eyes off the *freaking devil*.

The man leaned his head to the side, peering past Tristan to speak to Bryony. "This is rather sweet. Is he serious?"

"Yes, he is." Bryony sighed, pushing past Tristan and stepping in front of him again.

He was losing his mind. He wanted to grab her and yank her behind him where it was safe.

Except that was stupid. She wasn't safe behind him.

He couldn't protect her. He was no one here.

She was an angel. He'd seen what she did to Billy. He'd just get in her way.

Bryony barely glanced back at him. "He doesn't remember anything of his past life. Now he's just your normal, everyday human... but with Thurstan's face."

For some reason, that got him right in the gut, and his entire body felt hot with a weird shame he couldn't place.

Lucifer surveyed Tristan with an interested expression that unsettled him. He especially didn't like when the man's eyes flashed from dark—seemingly black—to bright red then back again.

"The memories are in there," Lucifer assessed.

Tristan jerked back. "What?"

"They're in your subconscious. I can see them." Lucifer tapped the side of his head. "You simply have to let your little human mind relax so your past can return to you."

Great. That didn't sound vague or complicated at all.

Lucifer stepped forward, oddly quick, hand

reaching out as though he meant to grab Tristan's throat.

Quick instinct took over. Without thinking, his hand reached back for the gun that had been tucked into his belt since Bryony had portaled them out of his apartment.

"Thurstan!"

"That's as far as you go, pal." Tristan shoved in front of Bryony again, raising his weapon and pointing it directly at the dark lord.

In the back of his mind, he knew this was ridiculous, but it was all he had. "Just tell us what you want."

Lucifer's thin, pale lips pulled apart in a wide grin, showing off the whites of his many pointed teeth. He laughed maniacally, taking another step.

Sweat beaded on the back of Tristan's neck. "Hey! I said stop! I will shoot you!"

Lucifer didn't stop, but the laughter did die, the smile melted away, and his eyes flashed that creepy red again.

With the next step, Tristan discharged his weapon.

Just once.

Aim for center mass. That was the rule. He was trained to hit, and it was most likely to put down a threat.

Except Lucifer didn't fucking flinch. He didn't

even blink his eyes. He didn't stumble back, didn't appear remotely hurt.

It took Tristan a moment to process what he'd just done.

He'd seen men shot multiple times and refuse to go down. In training videos, of course. They were usually a result of being high off their ass on some drug.

Or adrenaline.

This guy was as calm as could be. He wasn't high on anything. He wasn't breathing heavy.

He stared at Tristan as though they were playing a game he knew he was going to win.

I just shot Satan with a handgun, as if that was going to do anything. I'm a fucking idiot.

Lucifer straightened his tie and rolled his shoulders, and it was as though Tristan hadn't shot at all, though he'd heard his gun pop off, felt it buck in his hand, and now saw the gaping, steaming hole in Lucifer's pristine suit, right in the chest.

Tristan had treated shooting victims before. He'd asked one of them once what it had felt like. His patient had replied that getting shot was like getting punched real hard. Knocked the wind out of you.

But apparently not for Lucifer, who looked down at his suit, at the small hole, wiping his hand across it as though waving away the smoke.

"This is new," he said, cocking his head to the

side to look appraisingly at Tristan. "Last time we stood like this, you weren't so ready to go on the offensive."

"No?" Tristan asked, hoping the guy was more amused than angry.

Lucifer wet his lips. "Interesting."

Before anyone could reply, a searing hot, needle pain in Tristan's head forced him to drop his weapon and press his fingers to his temples as the pulsing hit him right behind the eyes.

"Lucifer! Stop!" Bryony shouted.

Tristan dropped to his knees, that thick spear digging down into his sinuses and nostrils until he couldn't breathe.

This happened before.

He, Bryony, Lucifer, and... so many others. They had been fighting at the time, and when they hadn't been fighting, they had been taunting each other. Different locations Tristan couldn't quite place, but it was them.

Bryony had been in front of him, with glorious golden wings, wearing... a strange ensemble that made her look like something out of a superhero movie.

Something lashed out at her. Tristan grabbed her, throwing her away, taking what had been meant for her.

The man had laughed as Thurstan crumbled. Bryony had cried.

And now Tristan thought he might be dying... again.

NINE

"Lucifer! Stop!" Bryony had to keep her attention on Lucifer. She glanced to Thurstan as he grabbed his head and dropped to his knees.

Her heart ached for him. She had the desire to get on her knees with him and do whatever she could to take his pain away.

She stiffened her spine and faced her enemy, hardening her heart to his pain as she focused on her target.

Maybe now he would stay out of the way and stop using feeble heroics.

As sweet as they might be, and as much as they reminded her of the old Thurstan, he really had no chance against their foe.

"He really is a human if he believes one of their

weapons would be effective against our kind." Lucifer brushed his chest. The hole disappeared, his suit knitting back together as though nothing had happened.

"What. Do. You. Want?" Bryony asked, enunciating each word between gritted teeth. She seethed at seeing Lucifer. *He* was the reason everything had been destroyed so long ago. *He* was the reason that Thurstan had been taken from her—and not even in an indirect *because he started the war* way, but in a *he directly killed Thurstan in front of her* way.

Four thousand years.

She'd almost allowed herself to forget.

Fuck this guy.

Bryony didn't lunge into an attack though. She wasn't sure what he had planned, and she was willing to wait a moment to try to find out before she did anything stupid—unlike Thurstan, who clearly now adhered to the human idea of *shoot first and ask questions later.*

She was pretty sure Lucifer didn't intend on killing them. He had no reason to. It wasn't like he was known for going around killing furies. He *could,* but the angels were strong, and it would take a terrible battle between them before he got the better of her.

"Him, of course." Lucifer gestured to Thurstan.

That was what she'd figured, and dreaded.

"What good is a human to you?"

He smiled that infuriating smile. "Can't you tell?"

Now that she thought about it, how had Lucifer found them so fast? There was no reason for him to be keeping tabs on her, yet he'd shown up the day after she'd found her long-lost love.

She glanced back at Thurstan. He was still on his knees, eyes dilated, sweat beading on his forehead.

And that was an improvement from a moment ago, at the very least.

Something bigger is going on here, Bryony thought, beginning to put the pieces together.

Lucifer barked a laugh, a chilling, terrifying sound that clearly affected Tristan, as he recoiled. Bryony stepped in front of him again so Lucifer wouldn't see a once-mighty angel cowering.

"Can you cut it out with your games for once?" she demanded. "What do you want from him?"

"I think my presence is perhaps a bit much for him," Lucifer said, ignoring her question yet again while peering past her at Tristan. "I must say I wasn't expecting him to be so... weak."

Bryony bristled, her hands clenching. "He is not weak."

"Oh? But you said yourself he's just a regular human, and by definition, humans are *weak.*"

She wasn't going to debate him. She would come

off sounding like a petulant child if she tried to say something like, *My man is strong for a human, though!*

Instead, she steered the conversation back to the point. "Is there something you wanted to discuss? Or did you only make a trip to Earth so that you might gaze at his rugged physique?"

"That was quite rude of you to portal out instead of answering the door," he said, once again ignoring the question. "And I was being polite by knocking instead of burning it down."

Typical Lucifer, playing mind games. Well, she could, too.

"Yeah, funny that. We were just leaving when we heard the knock and, you know, too lost in the glow of each other to pay much attention."

"Liar."

She was, but it didn't matter. She owed nothing to him.

"I don't appreciate your defiance, sweet Bryony."

She shivered in revulsion. She hated when he'd called her that when they were all in the heavens together, but now every time he said it, she wanted to punch him in the face.

"You're delusional if you think I owe you any obedience," she snapped. "Is the dark lord losing his mind, because you have no reason to think I would—"

Lucifer raised his hand and snapped his fingers.

Neither Bryony nor Thurstan had time to react.

Even if she'd had the time, she didn't know if she would have been able to move, because that sound, the snap of his fingers, it was identical to the noise that he'd made thousands of years ago, right before her world had ended, and it still terrified her to her core.

Bryony turned toward Thurstan as though moving in slow motion, watching an invisible force pulling him backward, sending him crashing into the far wall behind them.

The Thurstan she once knew could have stood through Lucifer's power. Could throw off anything like that without breaking a sweat.

Tristan, however, flew like a rag doll... like he was some kind of... human.

The crack of his spine was horrible and loud. He landed in a crumpled heap on the floor.

Bryony ran to him. "Thurstan!"

She fell to her knees next to him just as he tried to push himself up.

The fact that he could move at all, that his spine wasn't broken, was a heavy relief.

"What... what the fuck was that?" He coughed and groaned, already making a valiant attempt at pulling himself to his feet, but he barely made it to his knees before needing to lean on Bryony for support.

"Don't move." She was already looking him over, noting the deep red welt that would turn to purple bruising very soon on his face, wrapping around his shoulder and going down his arm. As though a giant hand had grasped him really tightly before flinging him away.

It could have been worse. Lucifer could tear a human to pieces if he wanted to. This was kid-glove stuff. Lucifer was giving them a little reminder of what he was capable of.

"How interesting," Lucifer said, stepping across his hall to approach Thurstan while he smiled, stroking his chin like the entire situation delighted him to no end. "You really *are* just a human. You got his pretty face, but no memories and no *strength*. Remarkable."

"Stay away from him," Bryony didn't care that Thurstan was human. He was still *hers,* and she would protect him until her dying breath.

She would *not* lose him again.

"Why would I—" Lucifer's next words were cut off by Bryony's fist striking his mouth.

His head snapped back, but he remained standing.

Bryony sucked in a breath, feeling stupid, and a little scared.

She'd been wanting to do that since... well... for four thousand years ago.

A punch like that would have killed a simple human, snapping their neck, breaking their teeth. Yet Lucifer wasn't even bloody as he stroked his jaw and then turned to look at her with those searing red eyes.

"Was that *really* necessary?"

She shrugged, not feeling overly confident about coming here anymore. "It felt good."

He needed to make no extra movements or motions to do what he wished to her.

Bryony suddenly couldn't move.

At first, she thought she couldn't breathe either, but she forced her panic down and managed to take small, shallow breathes while the dark lord's power held her frozen in place.

Lucifer walked a circle around her then stepped close. He pressed a hand to her forehead, sending his power coursing through her, a terrible vibration beneath her skin, inside her bones, and along every nerve traveling through her body, torturing her while she was incapable of screaming or writhing in pain.

The sudden shock of his power rushing through her felt so, *so* much worse than that time she had accidentally flown into power cables.

It felt worse than being struck by lightning—which she'd experienced *not* by accident, during a desperate time in her existence.

She wasn't even aware of when she'd been thrown backwards. Not until she crashed into the wall next to Thurstan.

Thurstan. She couldn't take a moment to recover from the blow. She had to get right up, to stay between Lucifer and Thurstan.

Lucifer looked bored when she stood before him, out of his reach this time. "You seemed to need a reminder of who you were talking to."

"Reminder received." The words came from Thurstan.

Bryony snapped her head toward him, watching him rise from the ground while she processed not only the words he'd just said but the change in tone and timbre of his voice.

He sounded... more like *Thurstan.*

"What do you mean?" she gasped, watching the way his glazed blue eyes moved from side to side, as though he were watching a scene unfold before him, a movie in his mind.

It couldn't be.

"Can you... are you..."

"I remember." His lips parted in shock, and he nodded. She heard it again, noted that his accent changed from modern American to more of their ancient lilt.

She gasped. This was what she'd wanted since she'd first spoken his name in the park the night before, but Thurstan seemed to be in pain, and not just from the blow Lucifer had dealt.

Thurstan touched his head again and winced. Bryony could only imagine what it felt like to recall everything—to be human and know nothing of any of this just to be thrown back into such a life. Once again, she wondered if the human brain was even equipped to handle the amount of knowledge that an angel held.

Perhaps it was Lucifer's show of power that was finally jarring it out of him. Bryony couldn't be sure, but she hated this was how he would remember.

Because she had no time to ask him if he was all right. He had to be. Because they were still facing off with Lucifer.

"I remember how *Lucifer killed me.*"

TEN

"You..." Thurstan took a breath, raising a hand to point at the dark lord. "You *killed* me."

Vaguely, he knew that his body ached, but physical pain meant nothing at the moment, because the weak Tristan body was the least of his concerns. He'd just come back to life and was facing the man who'd stolen a few millennia from him.

"You were always a little slow," Lucifer said, smiling back at Bryony. "Who would have thought it? He's finally returned. I spent so long wondering if Father would bring them back, since he likes to pretend he loves his children, after all. Do you think God did this? I figured that's what everyone would assume."

"I don't know, Lucifer," Bryony shot back, and

Thurstan could only figure that she was more annoyed now than ever, if she—like Thurstan—wanted the chance to have a moment with her lost love, instead of dealing with Lucifer. "Before we had any time to think about it, *you* were banging on the door."

"You don't know... hmm..." Lucifer shrugged. "Because if *I* were you, I would have been looking into that right away to make sure you pay proper thanks to the one responsible."

There it was. The reason Lucifer had popped up so soon after the reunion.

"*You* did this?" Bryony gasped, her eyes darting around, as though she was searching for an explanation. "You had him brought back to life to make us swear fealty to you. Seriously?"

Thurstan snorted. As if bringing him back now would be enough for them to forgive him.

"Ahh, where Thurstan was slow, you've always been quick. That *is* how he made all of you, isn't it? Two perfect halves to make a whole. It took you a few decades to find each other after his rebirth, but I am nothing if not patient."

Was he really taking this moment to wax poetic about how God hadn't given him a partner? Thurstan fumed.

Fuck this guy and his stupid loneliness.

"Was it just me?" Thurstan asked, though he felt he already knew the answer. Whatever effort Lucifer had taken to get one angel back to life wouldn't have been worth it. And since it took this long, he assumed that meant Lucifer must have been spending years readying whatever it took to reincarnate angel souls. "It's not, is it? You've gone all out, trying to create a new army for yourself. How many?"

"Unknown." He shrugged, and Thurstan got the impression Lucifer really wasn't sure what the correct answer was.

"I'm the first one," Thurstan realized.

Bryony's jaw dropped.

"You created a big scheme, planning to bring all these angels back, but you spent years not knowing if it worked!" Bryony actually laughed at him. Thurstan wouldn't have minded, if he wasn't still in a fragile human body that Lucifer could easily toss around.

Maybe let's not antagonize him, he thought, giving Bryony a look, hoping she'd get it.

She didn't. "No, you haven't known if it worked at all. All these years... and, Tristan, you're what, thirty?"

"My name is Thurstan," he replied. She finally looked at him, her eyes and mouth round in shock, which turned into the happiest of smiles as she really processed that he was back. "And I've spent thirty-five years in this human body."

"Thirty-five years." She turned back to Lucifer. "And you spent all that time not knowing if it worked! So you found the broken part of the pair—me—and had me followed until I met up with him."

"The world is a big place, full of billions of people," Lucifer replied. "Nearly four million born on Earth the year of my spell. No, sweet Bryony, I don't have the resources to watch every small baby grow into themselves. But I did have enough to follow those of you who left Heaven and now reside in the Underworld."

Thurstan's stomach churned. Lucifer had been watching Bryony. He was sure she must feel sick about it.

Lucifer continued. "The question is this: what side will you be on when the next war comes? My side will be stronger this time, and I will finally defeat Michael's army and take control of the heavens."

Bryony laughed. "That's only assuming the other furies find their lost lovers! If Thurstan is your only addition, that's just one extra. Not enough to—"

Lucifer cut her off. "You're right about one addition, but you're wrong about Thurstan. Again, as you said, Thurstan is just human. With or without his memories, he's no good to me on his own."

"She won't join you," Thurstan said, having figured out this angle before Lucifer himself got to it. "Gratitude alone isn't enough to make her swear allegiance to you. And we'll never forget that it was *you* that caused the war in the first place."

"But more importantly," Bryony added, "in *this* case, you personally felled Thurstan, and I will never forgive you for all the time I spent *alone* because of what you did."

Bryony allowed her wings to take shape, unfurling from her back into the warrior stance he'd seen her take only once—only during the War of Heaven when all angels were recruited for battle against Lucifer's legion.

She was breathtaking, but he didn't want to see her battle Lucifer one-on-one. She was no match for him. Only his brother, Michael, could truly kill him.

Supposedly.

"Stop," Thurstan shouted, grabbing her attention before he tried to push in front of Bryony yet again.

She refused to cede her spot. "You can't match him."

"Neither can you," he said.

"This is all very touching and sweet," Lucifer said. "But I have no intention of killing either of you. Yet."

"Because you think you'll somehow be able to

pull our strings when the time is right," Bryony guessed. "Think again. Our stance won't change."

"You know, sweet Bryony..." Lucifer chuckled while narrowing his eyes at her. "You've really become quite sure of yourself from all the time spent beating up *humans*"—he said the last word with distain—"and you seem to have forgotten what it's like to play with *someone like us.*"

He raised his hand, making a show of curling his fingers into a tight fist. Thurstan expected some kind of theatrics—a lightning bolt or the walls surrounding them bursting into flames, maybe—but he didn't expect to lose his ability to breathe.

CHAPTER

ELEVEN

Thurstan grunted, his hands clasping at his throat. Bryony spun to look at him, her heart stopping.

"Thurstan?"

He couldn't speak. He looked at her with a panic in his blue eyes, so similar to what she'd seen the day he took his last breath so long ago.

No. No. No.

He clutched his throat and chest, horrible wheezing noises pulling in and out of his mouth as he tried to force his breaths, falling to his knees.

"That's the lungs," Lucifer said as Bryony dropped down next to Thurstan, holding him. "I can play with anything I want. The heart maybe?"

Thurstan inhaled a heavy gasp before breathing

hard, as though he had been forced under water and just been let up.

But then his eyes widened in horror and he clutched his hands to his chest, his neck going tight, his face turning a bright shade of red.

"No!" Bryony shouted at Lucifer while she grabbed Thurstan's shoulders, searching his body for anything she could do to sever the hold Lucifer had on him.

There was no way. Lucifer's power was too strong. Her heart hammered with the possibility that she could lose Thurstan.

Again.

"Stop it!" she screamed, Thurstan's choked voice and gasps too much for her to bear. "Stop it!"

"You must understand, my sweet, this isn't just my power at work." He nodded toward Thurstan's pained face. "There is a tie between me and the angels I brought back. They're not my demons now, no, but as long as they maintain their human forms, their entire existence relies upon *my* desire for them to be here."

"Fine, I get it!" Bryony looked up to the ceiling and screamed. How great it would be if her Heavenly Father or Lucifer's brother, Michael, would help her. But of course they wouldn't. They wouldn't have even if she were still one of their soldiers. They hadn't the first time Lucifer killed Thurstan, and they wouldn't now.

"Do you get it?" Lucifer asked, while Thurstan fell from her arms and began to writhe on the ground, his face changing from red to a deep, horrible, ugly blue.

"Yes, I do. I definitely do," Bryony snapped, glaring at Lucifer. "You have the control, which means we're..."

"*Say it,*" Lucifer snarled.

"We're at your mercy, okay? We have to fight on your side during the war. We're your minions or whatever now, okay? I get it! I submit! Now *stop!*"

Lucifer opened his fist, and Thurstan lay still, no longer spasming, a heavy, wet breath sucking deeply into his lungs.

Bryony thought she might cry.

"Thurstan?"

He didn't seem to see her right away. His eyes blinked, and color returned to his face as his blood began circulating again.

"Oh my God," he moaned, his voice sounding like he'd just gargled hot coals. He took Bryony's hand, holding it weakly as she helped him back to his feet.

He leaned his whole weight against her, but she didn't care. He was warm and solid and alive. She didn't want to let him go.

"God abandoned us," Lucifer reminded, picking at his nails and flicking away something he dug out from under them. "As for what you will do for me..."

Bryony tensed. This was it. She'd fucked up. She said she would do anything, and now she would have to do it.

Anything to protect Thurstan.

"For the time being, I don't want much," Lucifer said, spreading his hands out. "I can be reasonable and only have a few small needs. I would not do something as terrible as kill a fury or her"—his lip curled up in a mocking smile—"*helpless* lover simply for a centuries-old grudge."

Except that was exactly the sort of thing Lucifer would do.

"I only ask that you stay out of the way," Lucifer said with a simple shrug. "I have business to attend to. You have been doing well enough with your human-hunting fun, chasing down those villains and bringing them to justice. Continue doing that, if you must pass the time, but"—he pointed a finger at her, his eyes flashing to red once more, and Bryony felt the pulsing of heat in the air around them—"you are to stay away from the others. No interference in my plans."

Bryony knew who he was talking about, and her blood boiled.

He was banning her from talking to her kind—

the other angels who'd left heaven and were no longer under God's control and hadn't sworn allegiance to Lucifer and become mindless zombies like Terry.

"Why? Because you don't want us all to team up against you?"

Lucifer's eyes narrowed to slits. "Like that would be a threat to me. No. I just don't want any interference. Your lot can be incredibly annoying when you want to be, but just remember who beat who the last time we all faced each other."

Lucifer's gaze flicked back to Thurstan. "Unless you want to go through that again."

Bryony clenched her hands. She *didn't* want to go through that again, and damn him, Lucifer knew that perfectly well.

"What exactly do you mean by no interference? You want me to make sure I don't cross paths with any of the other furies so they don't see Thurstan?"

"I don't care if they see Thurstan," Lucifer said with a shrug. "In fact, it would be good if they did. It would encourage their longing, and the more they long for love, the more likely their souls might take them to the right place at the right time to reunite with their lost lovers."

That was sick. That was so fucking disgusting Bryony couldn't stand it.

Bryony and Thurstan looked at each other. He

shrugged. Clearly he had no idea what Lucifer wanted them to do—or not do—either.

"So, what exactly does all of that—"

"You will take a binding oath with me," Lucifer said curtly. "It will prevent you from *speaking* to any of your kind before they've found their fallen angels. I don't want any interference that may fuck things up for me. It's a simple enough request, really. Stay out of it, stay away. If they come up and ask you about Thurstan, you don't say a word. You won't be able to, once you accept the deal."

"And after they find them?" Bryony asked, wondering exactly how much control Lucifer wanted over her.

"I couldn't care less if you talk to each other, then. I don't worry about anyone teaming up against me, because you know how easily I could take out your partner. So, talk all you want, once they're matched. It's not like you can conspire against me."

It was true.

In the grand scheme of things, he could demand so much worse from her, as well.

Bryony nodded, and reached out her hand. "I agree."

Lucifer grabbed it, his grip tight, searing, her skin burning as his eyes glowed red and they sealed the deal.

"Excellent."

TWELVE

Bryony portaled them out of Lucifer's castle, back to Tristan's apartment.

They were quiet for a moment, both of them hardly moving and Thurstan still leaning his body against hers.

"You didn't try to stop me from making the oath," Bryony said finally.

She didn't think he would hate her, but he had to be disgusted with her, especially if he remembered everything.

The other angels had been his friends, too.

Thurstan didn't answer. His blue eyes blazed, as if there was so much he wanted to say. Instead, he put his hand to the back of her head in a painful grip and kissed her.

Long, hard, and deep.

As if he needed to feel every inch of her.

Bryony got over her shock quickly, relieved and scared. She held him tight, kissing him back desperately.

A little sloppily, too, holding him close, her hands in his hair, relishing how she felt in his arms.

Praying she would be in them many times over after this.

When they separated with a gasp, he explained, "I know you, Bryony. I remember everything. Nothing I said could convince you otherwise, especially if I was telling you to sacrifice me."

She nodded, her heart full and hurting. Her eyes burning.

She really had her Thurstan back again.

Then the gravity of the deal settled on her. "I have to hope that day never comes when he stands against Michael again."

"It happened once. It will likely happen again. But hopefully we have time. Time to figure out how to break this connection Lucifer has to me."

"Do you think that's possible?" she asked, a bit of hope rekindling inside her.

She felt so small and helpless. She'd almost lost him again, watched as Lucifer tortured him.

She wouldn't sleep well tonight with Thurstan's blue face haunting her.

"I think it's worth looking into," he replied, though his mind didn't seem to be on that topic.

"Why are you smiling?"

"So, you're no longer an angel. You're a fury."

She frowned. "Yes. I told you." Had he forgotten that part when his memories flooded back? "Is that a problem for you?"

"No." He tugged her by the belt, a gleam in his eye. "You're hot."

She cocked her head to the side. "I don't think the Thurstan I knew so long ago was into black and leather. Or said words like *hot* in this context."

She liked it though. Her body was already beginning to feel warm.

"But I am a new Thurstan," he reminded her. "One with a combined personality and memories with a human I lived as for thirty-five years. Just as you're a new version of Bryony, who wears makeup but still gives great head."

"Oh God." She couldn't help but blush, feeling almost like she'd had sex with someone else the night before. "So you remember last night?"

"I remember *everything*." He brushed a strand of hair from her face. "And it breaks my heart to think of how long you had to live without me. And how when you finally saw me, you didn't know what to do to reintroduce yourself. I'm so glad my memories are back so you didn't have to live that long with me without them."

He inhaled a shaking breath. "I am so sorry I didn't remember you. I feel like I should have."

"It's okay." She pressed herself closer to him, holding him tightly. "It wasn't your fault."

He hugged her back, his chin resting on top of her head. "Feels like I should have. I feel...*ashamed* for not recognizing you."

"How do you feel about what I do now?" She pulled away, avoiding his gaze. "The fact that I dole out vengeance? The Thurstan I knew would have been disturbed that I'm doing that, much less liking it."

He sighed deeply, thick fingers pushing through her blonde hair. "I understand that a part of you has been irreversibly altered by my death and the years of life you had to live after I was gone." He stroked a hand down her face and pulled both her hands into his. "I understand that you've had to do whatever necessary to survive this long."

"Exactly," she breathed. "As angels, we turned a blind eye to the happenings on Earth. We let what was just be. But I couldn't do that anymore. When you were taken from me, and no one intervened, it stabbed me to the core. I could no longer turn a blind eye to the suffering of others."

She smiled softly. "And I liked to think I was

doing the work you would have done, if you'd been here."

"I understand," he assured her. "I'm not sure if I'll share that feeling, but I might. I do have that part of Tristan in my soul now, a part that is human and loyal to humanity, and he may want to work alongside you to bring justice to the world."

She nodded.

"I do have to wonder if part of you *is* grateful to Lucifer, though," Thurstan wondered, changing the subject. "It might be four thousand years later, but someone has done something, finally."

"Maybe," Bryony mused. "But he did it for his own ends. It wasn't altruistic. I have you back, but now I'm also enlisted in his army."

"And if all goes according to his plan, he'll have others. Other furies, like yourself. Are you in touch with them? Will they note a problem if you stop communication with them, as Lucifer wishes?"

"They won't notice anything, no," Bryony answered. "We've crossed paths. We're friendly, but not friends. We just were too alike to create good company for each other—angels too full of anger and pain to be good friends to one another."

She sighed, burrowing herself a little more deeply against Thurstan's chest. "At least, I was, I guess. The others, they were like widows of war and they had that in common. But for me, it felt more personal, since your death was directly at Lucifer's hands. It made it impossible for me to tolerate the other's moaning and complaining, when our pain wasn't the same. They didn't have one direct person to blame, like I did."

He looked down for a moment before admitting, "My question was more about... which other angels died back then?"

"Oh," She nodded, realizing there was still lots he didn't know, all that had taken place between Thurstan's death and Tristan's birth. Well, everything that Tristan couldn't have learned in school or from the internet. She took a deep breath before revealing to him which of his friends had died and were now probably back to life. "Ethan, Xander, and Oren, yes."

"And now they'll be like me if their memories return to them. They'll have the memories of being angels but reincarnated into human men with full human lives and frail human bodies, who are now owned by Lucifer."

"I guess so, yeah," Bryony agreed.

"It's almost like we *don't* want them to find each other," Thurstan realized. "Maybe *that* is why Lucifer didn't want us to communicate before they reunite. Because maybe the best thing is to allow us humans to live and die without ever knowing what we used to be. Without having to exist now in a lesser form, knowing we might have to see our loves sent off to Lucifer's war, as they had to watch us..."

"You can't mean that," she objected. "Not if you're the Thurstan I know."

"You're right." He pulled her into his arms. "I'd pay any price to be with you again. I just wish we could help the others."

She saw how tortured he was becoming at the thought and decided to put a stop to it for now. "You may be right, but there's nothing we can do about it now."

She remembered Thurstan writhing on the floor, unable to breathe, while Lucifer practically laughed. She couldn't let Lucifer kill Thurstan again. She didn't think she'd survive it.

"Well, what do we do now?" Thurstan asked.

"We live together, we enjoy each other," Bryony suggested. "I went so long without you. I don't want to waste time on *anything* else."

"First off, we never were that kind of couple— that sounds a little clingy," he joked. "Second, I'm mortal. So even if Lucifer doesn't do away with me, I still have a limited number of days on this—"

"Don't." Bryony held up her hand to stop him. "Don't say it."

He gently took hold of her hand, lowering it. "Baby, let's say we get sixty years together. Wouldn't you rather we have more?"

"More?" Bryony blinked, trying to understand his line of thinking. "I don't think breaking Lucifer's hold would stop you from... old age..."

Though it was a nice idea.

"But what if we find the rest of me?" he asked, his eyes shining with excitement and hope. "Everything that makes us who we are simply changes form when we die. Lucifer's spell pulled my soul into this body, but the rest of me, the power that I had, which I'm now missing, is out there. What if we can find it, harness it, reunite it with my soul in this body?"

She didn't know if that was true. Thurstan could be just taking a wild stab at an unlikely possibility, but that was fine. If he wanted to spend his human life searching for something that might not really exist, she'd do it with him. Anything, as long as they were together. Whatever made him happy.

Even if she had to watch him become a little old man someday. She'd still love him, and she'd take care of him to his dying breath. It would be better than Lucifer ripping him away from her again.

Though her heart wrenched at the thought of seeing him die a second time.

Thurstan touched her chin, guiding her to look at him. "I was a healer, remember?" he asked, his eyes shining with hope. "I *know* these things. What

I'm suggesting isn't a wild goose chase. It's something possible."

"The others should know too, then. If they reunite." She thought about Thurstan's assessment —that the humans might be better off if they never realized who they really were. Was he right?

It didn't matter. There was nothing they could do about it, not if they wanted to avoid Lucifer's wrath.

Besides, the oath they took meant they *literally* couldn't speak to the others, even if they tried. No words would come out.

"We do the research," Thurstan continued. "We figure out where to start. And then, if the others reunite, we'll have a starting place for them to join us. We're not letting Lucifer get the better of us. Not that easily."

Bryony's smile faded with a final thought. "How do we know your human body will accept your angel essence?"

"We don't." He stroked her face. She could see the determination in his eyes. "But we'll do all we can to figure it out."

Bryony swallowed hard, her throat closing. "Together?"

Even after everything Lucifer had said and done, and what he wanted her to do, having Thurstan with her, knowing they weren't giving up, eased the burden of what was coming.

"Yes, together," Thurstan said, kissing her in the warm sunlight that streamed in through his window.

The End.

ALSO BY MANDY ROSKO

PARANORMAL ROMANCE

Blood Secrets

Darkness Awakened

Passion Awakened

Eve Langlais' FUCN'A

I'll Be Dammed

Trash Queen

Chillin' Out

Bits and Bobs

Goddesses of Vengeance

Angel's Fury

You've Got to be Shifting Me

Zero Fox Given

Howl Always Love You

Can't Bear to Be Without You

Alpha Bites

Alpha

Alpha Bear

Alpha Dragon

Alpha Wolf

Dangerous Creatures

Burns Like Fire

A Shock to Your System

As Cold as Ice

Gonna Make You Howl

Things in The Night

The Vampire's Curse

The Legend of the Werewolf

The Shepard's Agony

The Dragon and The Wolf

Night and Day (M/M)

Night and Day

Calm Before the Storm

All Hell Breaking Loose

Stand-alone PNR

Clockwork Heart

Jessie's Harem

Kidnapped by the Dragon

Bad Boy Bear

The Wild Wolf's Wife

Vampires Don't Share with Dragons

The Vampire and the Dragon's Christmas

Dangerous Guardian

Mate of a Dragon Villain

Bite Me

Sold to the Enemy

The Princess' Dragon Lord

The Princess and the Dragon's Holiday

My Angel Lover Have Mercy on Me (M/M)

CONTEMPORARY ROMANCE

Bad Boy Billionaire Brothers

Arrangement with a Billionaire

Holiday with a Billionaire

The Billionaire's Fantasy

HISTORICAL ROMANCE

Lady Deception

Lady Thief

Learn more at mandyrosko.com

ALSO BY RENEE HEWETT

FURRY UNITED COALITION NEWBIE ACADEMY

Goose and the Ocelot

Moose and the Narwhal

GREENVILLE VAMPIRES

Short stories

Mistletoe and Vampires

The Vampire's Black Jack

ABOUT MANDY ROSKO

USA Today Bestselling Author Mandy Rosko is a video game playing, book loving chick. She loves writing paranormal romances that range from light steamy to erotic, and has some contemporary and historical romances as well. You can find her on all sorts of platforms, including Twitch, where she does writing sprints, crafting, and video gaming!

Get all the latest news from Mandy by signing up for

her newsletter: subscribepage.com/mandy-roskobooks

As a bonus for signing up, you'll get her starter library, including Burns Like Fire, Sold to the Enemy, and The Vampire's Curse!

facebook.com/MandyRoskoRomance
instagram.com/mandyroskodraws
amazon.com/Mandy-Rosko/e/B008ETBVFW
bookbub.com/authors/mandy-rosko
goodreads.com/mandyrosko
youtube.com/UCD1z6r06dKoN-0WdUbi1pAQ

ABOUT RENEE HEWETT

Renee Hewett writes paranormal romance. Many of these stories are in shared worlds, including Milly Taiden's MT Worlds, Eve Langlais' EveL Worlds, and Crimson Moon Hideaway. Before becoming a full-time writer she worked in marketing, web writing, and editing. She's volunteered for at many events, such as C4 Comic Con, Can-Con, and Romancing the Capital.

ReneeHewett.com
Facebook reader group
Sign up for Renee's Newsletter

facebook.com/ReneeHewettauthor

twitter.com/reneehewettpnr

instagram.com/reneehewettauthor